The Road to Canada

Book four of
Girls of Summer

by Kate Christie

SECOND GROWTH

Copyright © 2019 by Kate Christie

Second Growth Books
Seattle, WA

All rights reserved. No part of this book may be reproduced or transmitted in any form or by any means, electronic or mechanical, including photocopying, without permission in writing from the author.

This is a work of fiction. Names, characters, organizations, events, and incidents are either the products of the author's imagination or used in a fictitious manner. Any resemblance to actual organizations, persons (living or dead), events, or incidents is purely coincidental.

Printed in the United States of America on acid-free paper
First published 2019

Cover Design: Kate Christie

ISBN-13: 978-1-7977999-1-9

DEDICATION

To the '15ers: Thanks for inspiring a nation of women and girls to reach for our dreams—and to fight for equality, both on and off the pitch.

ACKNOWLEDGMENTS

Many thanks to the able Margaret Burris, copy editor extraordinaire. Any errors contained in the following pages are mine, likely the result of last-minute changes I know I shouldn't make but can't seem to stop myself from doing—*just one more tiny edit…*

CHAPTER ONE

Jamie tried to blink away the sweat dripping into her eyes. She would have used her hands, but they were currently occupied.

"That's it," Emma said, her voice urgent. "Don't stop, Jamie!"

Breathing hard, Jamie closed her eyes and narrowed her focus. She wasn't about to stop now, not with Emma urging her on. Besides, the burn in her muscles was only lactic acid.

Above her, Emma's voice rose in pitch. "Come on, Jamie. That's it. Yes!"

Jamie strained, concentrating her energy on one task. She could do this. Just a little more…

Another voice broke in. "Gross, you guys. Keep your sex talk to yourselves!"

Jamie's eyes flew open, and she glared at Angie as fiercely as she could muster while lying on her back. "Dude. Fuck off."

Angie smirked. "That's what she said."

A white towel snapped and caught Angie in the ass, and Jamie grimaced in a grin of sorts as her friend squealed in pain.

"I can't believe you did that," Angie said, scowling over her shoulder.

"You know you love it," Maddie replied.

"Ew," Emma said, shaking her head. "And I did not need to hear that."

"Serves you right," Jamie grunted at Angie. She glanced up at Emma. "How many is that?"

"Nine," Emma told her, hands extended, ready to catch the bar if Jamie needed assistance.

"Three more," Jamie said, gritting her teeth as she prepared to lift the bar again.

"You can do it," Emma coached. "You got it."

Around them, their teammates worked individually and in pairs, moving through the machines and other stations as prescribed by the national team's fitness staff. Lacey Rodriguez and her assailan—*assistants* were pacing the weight room on the lookout for cheating reps and improper form, their sharp eyes missing nothing. Except, Jamie hoped, Angie's wildly inappropriate comments. At least her January camp roommate had waited until no one else but their girlfriends were around to crack one of her many tasteless jokes.

Two weeks into the twenty-day residency camp, Jamie felt like she'd spent more time in the gym and on the track than on the soccer field. She now understood why the veterans on the team referred to January camp as "Death Camp." During the opening meeting the first night, Lacey had joked that they were all going to hate her when they saw what she had in store for them, but Jamie hadn't realized just how intense the off-field workouts would be.

Still, none of them would be here if they didn't enjoy pushing their bodies to the point of almost breaking. Lacey sent out regular training updates throughout the year with sample training plans and information on the program's semi-annual fitness testing, so it was your own fault if you came into camp unfit. Jamie had been around the youth and senior national teams long enough to know that you would be sent packing if you allowed your sprint times or endurance to drop off during downtime away from the team.

Maybe that was why the coaching staff had taken the team to Brazil in December: so that no one would be tempted to take an extended break from their fitness routine. Like any of them would. It was a World Cup year, for eff's sake, and they had something to prove. The international rankings had come out in December after they lost to Brazil, and for the first time since 2007, the US had dropped to second place in the world behind Germany. That meant they would almost certainly have to do better than the German side in Canada to regain the top slot.

At the same meeting where Lacey had apologized in advance for the fitness torture she was about to inflict, an unusually serious Jo Nichols had stood at the front of the conference room, flanked by her unsmiling assistants as she gazed around the room. "There are twenty-nine of you here," she had said, briefly making eye contact with each player, "but only twenty-three can make the World Cup roster. That means we need to see the absolute best you can give us, athletes. That means each of you needs to elevate your game. That means you need to come to every single training session prepared to give your best. You control your own destiny. We can give you the tools to succeed, but ultimately you're the one who decides what you do with those tools."

Now, as Jamie struggled to lift the bar, stacked with more weight than she was accustomed to lifting, she could feel the seductive lure of negativity. Six people would be cut between now and the spring when the official roster was announced, and the only roster she'd managed to make in the past year was for Brazil. She'd made the cut then, but they'd taken twenty-four players to South America. Twenty-four—one more than the World Cup roster allowed.

What if she was the last player cut before Canada? How would she ever face her friends and family—and Emma—again?

"You can do it," Emma said, smiling down at her. "One more, Jamie. You got it."

Jamie took a deep breath and closed her eyes again, focusing her energy on her hands, arms, shoulders, and abs. Teeth clenched, she pushed up, muscles burning, arms trembling.

"You got it," Angie added, followed by Maddie's encouraging, "Get it, Max!"

And—*there!* She'd done it.

Emma reached out and helped her guide the bar back onto the rack. "I knew you could do it."

"That makes one of us," Jamie joked, sitting up on the bench and wiping the sweat from her face at last.

She sat for a moment, catching her breath and reminding herself to take the journey one step at a time, one day at a time. Less than a year ago she had been cut from the program, and now here she was with a credible shot at making the World Cup roster. THE WORLD CUP ROSTER. If that didn't show what was possible, she wasn't sure what did.

"My turn," Emma said, stretching her arms over her

head. Her shirt rose with the movement, revealing a tanned swath of muscled midsection.

"Totally." Jamie bit her lip as she rose from the bench. Team time. Professionalism. *Totally.*

#

The afternoon session later that day took place outdoors at the National Training Center's practice fields and centered on one of Jamie's favorite parts of the game: set pieces. It could have been ninety minutes of one v. one defensive drills and sprint training and she still would have been happy to be in the warm Southern California sunshine instead of the smelly, fluorescent-lit interior of the weight room. Fitness training, as far as she as concerned, was a necessary evil of the game. Lofting perfectly weighted corner kicks into the box for her teammates to run onto, on the other hand, was a definite perk of the job.

Practice was almost over when Jo called her over to discuss her ball placement on free kicks.

"When we're within our offensive third, I'd like you to look for Ellie," Jo said, turning Jamie with a hand on her shoulder and gesturing toward the goal where Ellie, Jenny, and a handful of other offensive players were taking shots on Phoebe and Avery. Trish and Britt, the third and fourth string keepers respectively, were at the other end of the field working with the keeper coaches.

Or, at least, they had been.

"Just Ellie?" Jamie asked, frowning a little. "Because I thought you said—" She stopped as Britt popped out from behind her and, before Jamie could react, pushed a whipped cream pie into her face.

"Happy birthday, James!" Britt crowed, laughing.

What the fuck? Jamie shoved blindly at her friend with

one hand while wiping away—*was that Cool Whip?*—whipped cream with the other. "Jackass," she choked out, but she was laughing, too, because with this team, the ambush could have been much, much worse. Although, now that she thought of it, was Cool Whip even on the approved team diet? Probably she'd better steer clear of Lacey and Bianca, the team's nutritionist.

"And with that," Jo said, her tone amused, "I think practice is over. Happy birthday, Maxwell."

"Thanks, Coach," Jamie said, still wiping whipped cream from her cheeks and eyebrows.

"Hey," Angie said, slinging an arm around her waist, "are you ready for some dancing? Because I think Ellie said something about mandatory team bonding tonight…"

If she were being honest, mandatory team bonding was not how Jamie would have chosen to spend the evening. When the coaches had mentioned at lunch that the team would have the following day off, she and Emma had exchanged a hopeful look. Maybe they would actually be able to celebrate her birthday on their own. But then Phoebe and Ellie had squashed that plan with their whole captains' shtick, and now Jamie and Emma would be celebrating with the entire team en masse.

Which might not be a bad thing, really. Jamie vividly remembered her last January camp, right before Craig cut her from the program. Going out with the team hadn't stopped her and Emma from holding hands under the table at the club Ellie and Phoebe had chosen for their team outing. She doubted it would stop them from making ou—*ahem*, from hanging out tonight, either. But first, she needed a shower to wash off the cream pie.

And yeah, that wasn't a line she had ever expected to think.

A few hours later, Jamie glanced toward the dance floor, wondering if she should cut in between Emma and Jenny, who were laughing it up after a round of shots. *Nah.* She was just being selfish. Emma and Jenny were clearly having fun, and it wasn't like Jamie and Emma hadn't spent time together that night. Just like on previous occasions, the team had eaten dinner at a large eatery with a back room that could accommodate thirty people. This time, though, Jamie had sat at the same table as Emma and Ellie. No more Ellie making creepy spying gestures between Jamie and Maddie, no more guzzling wine with newbies. She was now routinely hanging out with veteran stars even though she had fewer than a handful of caps to her own name and, as Jo had pointed out on New Year's Day, was squarely on the bubble for the World Cup.

After dinner, they'd driven the team vans to the same dance club they'd patronized previously, where confirmed party girl Jenny Latham had insisted on a round of birthday shots. Jamie had declined, but Emma hadn't. Afterward, those who wanted to dance had gone straight to the dance floor while those who didn't—Ellie, Gabe, and Jamie, to name a few—ordered nachos, fries, and other food that was most definitely not on the approved team diet list. One night wouldn't hurt, would it?

Unexpectedly, Jamie missed the previous year's birthday celebration. She and Emma had sat pressed up against each other in one of the semi-circle booths, holding hands and flashing secret smiles at each other while a very pregnant Tina Baker had chatted with Ellie, Steph, and Phoebe. They weren't officially together yet, but Emma couldn't seem to stay away from her. Tonight, though, she was having no problem keeping her distance. She'd sat across from Jamie at dinner, and now she was out on the dance floor, sandwiched between Jenny and Maddie, apparently content to share an occasional look while maintaining the separation US Soccer demanded.

"Yo, Max," Gabe said, flicking her in the bicep.

"Ow. What the hell, man?"

Gabe rolled her eyes at Ellie as if to say, *Can you believe this idiot?*

"Why don't you just go dance already?" Ellie asked.

"Fine." Jamie grabbed the last of the nachos from the platter and jammed them in her mouth, leaving the booth to a chorus of boos.

She planned to join Emma and her group of friends, but then Britt and Angie waved her over, and Lisa and Rebecca were there too, and anyway, Jamie and Emma weren't exactly an old married couple. They could dance with other people, couldn't they?

Only, she thought a few minutes later as she moved to the beat and tried to avoid Britt's elbows, this wasn't really where she wanted to be right now. She had hoped she and Emma might find some time to themselves tonight, especially since it was their first time spending either person's birthday in the same city since they'd become a couple. They'd been on different continents in October for Emma's big day—a freezing, closet-encumbered occasion Jamie preferred not to dwell on—and though they'd talked to each other on their birthdays back in high school, they had never been in each other's physical presence. Until now.

She caught Emma's eye once again, and once again her girlfriend smiled at her before turning her attention back to Jenny. As Jamie watched Jenny take Emma's hands and spin her around laughingly, she tried to push down a wave of envy. Stupid US Soccer and their stupid professionalism clauses. At least they'd gotten a chance to celebrate that morning. Emma had taken her out to breakfast, where she'd presented Jamie with a gift certificate for tickets to *Pitch Perfect 2*, due to open in May. They'd spent most of the day together, and yet thanks to team rules, Emma seemed more like just another friend than her long-term girlfriend. And yes, Jamie knew she was behaving a bit like an entitled douche, but she had been trained since early childhood to think of this day as the one twenty-four-hour period each year when she got to embrace her own inner selfishness.

The team stayed out until close to curfew, and Emma remained tantalizingly out of reach. She didn't even sit next to Jamie in the van on the way back to the hotel. Jamie spent the ride squished between Angie and Britt, lamenting the fact that she was sober, more exhausted than she'd been in what felt like years, and the arms around her shoulders belonged to her best friends instead of her girlfriend. And yet, she reminded herself, she was at training camp with the national team and so was Emma. Wasn't that birthday present enough?

Gabe, Emma's camp roommate, flashed them a knowing smile when the group reached Jamie and Angie's room first. Angie and Maddie slapped hands—they were planning to go out for breakfast the following morning, Jamie knew—and then Angie tugged Emma toward the room with a breezy, "Come on, Blake. I've got that medicated rub you wanted."

Jamie saw Ellie's brow lift, and yes, the phrase did sound indecent, but it wasn't like teammates didn't routinely share their pain-relief secrets, she thought as she followed Angie and Emma into the room, closing the door securely behind them.

"Tick, tock, mothafuckas," Angie said as she slipped

into the bathroom, her phone in hand. "Don't say I didn't give you a present this year, Jamieson." The door shut and the bathroom fan went on, and seriously? Was Angie scrolling through Instagram or was she actually…?

Never mind. Jamie didn't want to know.

Emma grabbed her hand and tugged her to the bed by the window. "Was this your idea?" she asked as she pulled Jamie down onto the comforter cover.

"No," she admitted. "I thought it might be yours." She held herself still as Emma leaned in to kiss her neck, blinking up at the ceiling.

After a moment, Emma paused and levered herself up on her elbow. "Are you too tired for this?"

"Probably." But it wasn't that. She could tell Emma the truth, couldn't she? "It's just, you seemed really distant tonight. Like, all night."

"Oh." Emma pulled back even more. "Well, we sort of have to be, don't we?"

Jamie gazed up at her. "We could have at least danced near each other. I mean, Jenny was legitimately dry-humping you for half the night, Emma."

Her girlfriend's head tilted. "Are you jealous of Jenny?"

"No," Jamie said, and then let out a frustrated breath. "The word is envious. She got to touch you and I didn't."

"She's not touching me now," Emma pointed out. Her hand slid across Jamie's collared shirt and rested on her belt as she leaned in and whispered, "Besides, I would much rather you touch me, Jamie. You know that."

Jamie's breath hitched at the light pressure on her belt buckle. Why was she pouting when she wouldn't have Emma in her bed much longer? That was the challenge of team time: to make the most of their brief alone time. Besides, it wasn't Emma's fault they couldn't show PDA around the team, not even on their birthdays.

She turned her head so that their lips brushed lightly. "I would much rather that, too."

"Good," Emma murmured against her mouth. Then she maneuvered on top of Jamie and slipped one leg between hers. "Guess we better make this fast, hmm?"

An in-person quickie was so much better than skexing from a thin-walled closet in a dank North London basement apartment, Jamie thought a short time later when Emma flopped down next to her again, breathing hard. So. Much. Better.

"Happy birthday," Emma whispered, kissing the corner of her mouth.

"Happy—I mean, thanks," Jamie whispered back, smiling besottedly.

Angie, of course, had to ruin the moment by opening the door a crack and saying, "Are you finished? 'Cause it sounds like you're finished."

"Fuck off, Angie!" Jamie whisper-shouted.

"That's what she said," Angie replied for the second time that day. "Seriously, though, it's curfew, birthday girl. You have one minute to cover up your birthday suit."

The door shut again, and Jamie sighed. "Sorry about that."

"It's okay. Without Angie, I wouldn't have gotten to do this." She leaned in to kiss Jamie one last time before slipping from the bed.

Jamie followed, and they smiled sheepishly at each other as they pulled on their hastily shed clothing. Emma was patting down her hair as she headed to the door, Jamie on her heels, when she glanced back and said, "Gabe is meeting her family for breakfast tomorrow morning. What do you think about having coffee in my room?"

Tomorrow was their rest day, which meant they could spend it any way they wanted. Jamie paused, her hand on the doorknob as she pictured coffee and tea and the Premier League Match of the Day in Emma's room. *Naked.* Yep, this birthday weekend was definitely looking up.

"I think that sounds perfect," she said, smiling.

"Good. I'll text you tomorrow when it's all clear." Emma pecked her on the cheek. "Happy birthday, Jamie. I'm glad we got to spend it together."

"Me, too," Jamie said. And then she opened the door a crack and watched as Emma disappeared into the hallway. If they were lucky, Jessica North wouldn't happen to be walking by and observe Emma's flushed cheeks and obvious sex head. The coaches, either, for that matter.

The bathroom door opened. "You're welcome," Angie said, grinning. "Now take a shower, will you?"

"Whatever," she said, and brushed past her friend, ignoring her laughter. She wasn't really mad at Angie, though. After all, the other woman had made sure she didn't end her birthday orgasm-free.

Ten minutes later, she slipped between her sheets and reached for her Kindle. In the opposite bed, Angie was sitting up against her own pillows, iPad in hand.

"What are you watching?" Jamie asked.

"*Chicago Fire*," Angie said, and pulled off her headphones. "Maddie loves it, so I thought I would give it a try. What about you? Fan fiction or Netflix?"

"I haven't decided yet."

"You okay? You seemed a little quiet at the bar."

"I'm fine. It's just, team time sucks, doesn't it?"

"I don't know." Angie shrugged. "I thought it did, but now I sort of think it's more for protection than persecution. I mean, as long as we abide by the policy, no one can come after us for being involved with a teammate. At least, no one connected to the federation, anyway."

Her wording seemed significant. "What do you mean, no one connected to the federation?"

"Oh." Angie's eyes flickered, and she fumbled with her headphones. "Nothing, really. It doesn't mean anything. I have to finish this episode, okay? Happy birthday, Max."

"Thanks," she said automatically, and turned back to her own tablet as Angie refocused on her iPad.

Her finger hovered over the Netflix icon, but then she moved it away. She didn't feel like starting anything new. It usually took her forever to decide what to watch, and it was getting late. Twitter would be a double-edged sword: birthday messages from fans and less pleasant tweets from trolls. There had been a lot of those lately, some of them downright disturbing, but it wasn't like she was the only female athlete receiving them. That left one good option: fan fiction and its perfect, homophobia-free alternate worlds.

She was still searching through tags on the Archive of Our Own website when her phone buzzed. She picked it up from the bedside table, squinting as she saw Emma's name. "Happy birthday again, Jamie," she had texted, followed by a link to a website Jamie didn't recognize. Studio Byzantine? What even was that? But it was from Emma, so it probably wasn't virus-laden… She clicked the link and ended up on a website for a tattoo parlor in

Seattle.

Her phone buzzed again with an incoming Skype call from Emma.

"Dude," Jamie answered, laughing as she tucked her ear buds into place, "what did you just send me?"

"I'm sorry—I was going to wait until tomorrow but I couldn't!" Emma said, smiling. She was dressed in her sleep shirt, and with her hair down and face scrubbed free of makeup, she barely looked 20. "You said you wanted a tattoo of that tree on your calf, so I thought maybe I could give it to you."

"You're such a dork. A dork who gives awesome presents," Jamie amended as Emma huffed at her from five rooms away.

"I considered surprising you when we got home, but this is the first time we've ever been together on your actual birthday, and I wanted it to be special. Well, as special as it could be at Death Camp."

"It was," Jamie said, her voice softening. "It really was. I'm glad I got to spend it with you, Emma."

"Me, too, Jamie," Emma said, smiling at her through the airwaves.

And yes, it was a little bit ridiculous that they had to spend the night apart. After all, they were consenting adults in a committed relationship. But this was the life they had both chosen. And honestly, Jamie wouldn't trade it for anything.

Emma, she was pretty sure, wouldn't either.

"Thank you," Jamie said. "I love it, and I love you."

"I love you, too." Emma flashed a jaunty wink. "Thanks for earlier."

"Um, pretty sure I'm the one who owes you the

thanks."

"You can finish what we started in the morning," she promised.

As much as Jamie had enjoyed her seven minutes of pillow queendom earlier, more time together in the morning was a much better option to look forward to. "Can't wait."

"Same," Emma said. "Love you, birthday girl. Especially in your birthday suit."

"Ditto. Now, get some sleep, huh? I'll see you in the morning."

"Yes, you will." Emma blew her a kiss that Jamie pretended to catch and tuck under her pillow, and then they were hanging up, still laughing at each other's cheesiness even as the screen winked out.

Jamie turned off her phone and the lamp over her bed, snuggling down into her bed with the tablet beside her. But she didn't turn it on. Instead she closed her eyes and pictured the tree design she'd finally perfected, the one she wanted to add to her body to remind her to stay grounded in this, the year that had the potential to be the second hardest of her life. That, or the best ever. Either way, it wouldn't be easy. As she'd told Emma's family over the holidays, one way or the other she would be at the World Cup.

Could she really cheer on Emma and the others if she didn't make the cut? She wasn't sure. She hoped she wouldn't have to find out.

"You calling it a night?" Angie asked.

Jamie opened one eye and squinted at her friend. "Yep."

"'Kay. Goodnight, Jamie."

"Goodnight, Angie."

Down the hall, she pictured Emma arranging the covers on her bed in the room she shared with Gabe, pictured her setting her ear plugs in place and reaching for her eyeshade. Soon enough, morning would come and they would be alone together for a few blessed hours. And that, really, was the best birthday present Jamie could ask for.

CHAPTER TWO

Emma touched the ball once and sent it straight up the field to Jamie. Then she moved into a supporting position and called for the return pass. Immediately, Jamie dropped the ball back to her on an angle. Before the pass arrived, Emma lifted her head to assess her options—Ellie was calling for the ball inside the penalty box, but she had a defender on her back. Angie was open outside, though, so Emma one-touched it to her. The midfielder took the pass in stride and drove to the end line before rocketing a cross back into the center. As she had done too many times in a national team uniform to count, Ellie skied above her defender and buried the ball in the back of the net.

"Sweet!" Ellie called, turning away from the goal to give Emma a thumbs-up. "That was good. But let's try it again, and this time, pass the ball to my feet when I ask for it, okay?"

Emma nodded and jogged back into place. She *had* considered passing to Ellie in traffic, but her mind almost always chose the safer route, the sure pass. As a defender, she was more concerned with maintaining possession than attacking. Frankly, she'd rather hit the open player on the outside than risk missing the more dangerous player inside the box.

Jo claimed that players with a more defensive outlook suffered from a fear of failure. Playing it safe, she liked to say, stifled creativity. Of course, she was a former striker herself, so she would say that, wouldn't she? As an offensive-minded former player, Jo valued that same trait in the athletes she coached. She wanted everyone on the field to have an attacking mentality, to get forward and take risks. That was the mindset she had tasked Emma with developing. And while Emma may not agree with Jo's approach, she wanted to play. That was why she'd asked the best offensive players she knew for help.

Throughout the final week of January camp, Ellie, Jamie, Maddie, Angie, and Jenny had stayed after training with her to run extra passing patterns, to work on movement off the ball, and to practice variety in the attacking third: one player checking, one penetrating, and one shifting back on the weak side to provide balance in the back field. They had practiced getting to the end line and slotting a variety of services into the box: near post on the ground, far post in the air, top of the box both on the ground and in the air, and Jamie's favorite, a drive into the eighteen followed by a "cheeky" chip to the far post. Even though she normally didn't think much about attacking, Emma challenged herself during these drills, looking for Ellie's head when she was the crosser and focusing on placing the ball in the net with whatever part of her body was handiest when she was on the receiving end.

The most important building block of offensive play, Jo had said more than once, was technical skill—precision in passing, dribbling, and shooting combined with overall confidence on the ball. For defenders moving forward into the attack, that translated into serving good passes and always remaining calm on the ball, no matter where you might find yourself on the field.

"If you don't believe you can do something," Jo could be heard calling out across the National Training Center's practice fields at least once a day, "then you won't be able to do it."

That was probably how US Soccer's marketing arm had come up with the motto for the 2014 World Cup: "I believe that we will win." A Naval Academy student may have made the chant popular at sporting events in the late '90s, but Emma suspected that Jo's repeated use of the motivating cheer had influenced US Soccer's adoption of the phrase as an official rallying call for both the men's and women's teams.

As Emma dribbled back into place, she took a deep breath. She could do this. She totally could. With a nod to her friends, she started forward again. This time she touched the ball outside to Maddie before checking back for it. Maddie returned the ball and Emma dribbled forward again. No more than three touches—that was the rule for today's drill. Touch, touch, and pass. They repeated the earlier pattern: Emma to Jamie, and Jamie back to Emma. Only this time, as Ellie checked toward her, Emma was ready. She touched the ball to Ellie's feet and watched as Ellie used her defender's momentum to roll off and around her at the 12. Then she rocketed the ball into the net, which snapped resoundingly with the force of her shot.

"There," Ellie called, grinning at her. "See? You gave me a perfectly weighted pass right where I needed it to juke my defender."

"Yeah," Emma said, tilting her head, "but isn't it a stretch to call J-La a defender?"

Jenny placed her hands on her hips in mock outrage.

"Excuse you, but I have improved literally a hundred percent in my defensive takeaways!"

"So what, you're up to two per game now?" Emma asked, biting her lip as Jenny pretended to vibrate in anger. "Just kidding. Seriously, thanks, you guys, but I think we should probably call it a night. Don't want to miss dinner."

Everyone agreed whole-heartedly, and they set about collecting the extra balls and storing them back in the equipment area. Then they headed out to the parking lot where Ellie had left "her" van that afternoon. Lunchtime seemed so far away. Emma wanted only to eat two helpings of whatever meal the nutritionist had concocted, take a hot shower, and watch crappy television with Jamie and their friends until curfew. With only a few days of camp left to go, she was deeply, truly tired. She was looking forward to the week off between camp and the upcoming trip to Europe where they would play France and England, the number three and number six teams in the world, respectively. If all went well, she and Jamie would both go.

Fingers crossed.

An hour later, she was still toweling her hair dry when a soft knock sounded at the door. "Come in," she called.

Jamie poked her head around the edge of the door. "Are you decent?"

"Unfortunately." Gabe was gone for now but there was no telling when she would return, which meant they would have to be on their best behavior. Or at least good behavior, anyway. It wasn't like either of them were rooming with Jessica North this time around, but Emma didn't want to make Gabe uncomfortable. She didn't like the idea of asking their teammates to cover for them. Jamie's birthday had been one thing—one very enjoyable thing—but regular residency camp life? Not so much.

"Bummer," Jamie commented, and strolled in, cheeks pink and hair damp from her own recent shower.

Soon they were stretched out on the bed beside each other, backs against the pillows, hands clasped loosely as Emma flicked through the channels. Her room meant her remote, a rule they adhered to even more closely than they did to US Soccer's team time policy.

"Hockey?" she asked.

Jamie made a face.

"Basketball?"

"Who's playing?"

"Does it matter?" As Jamie gazed at her, one eyebrow lifted meaningfully, she sighed and squinted at the screen. "Michigan State and Penn State." The game had just started, which meant it had to be a replay, given the time difference on the East Coast.

Jamie shrugged. "That's fine. I'm more interested in hearing about your meeting with Caroline, anyway. What did she have to say?"

Emma kept her eyes on the television. If she looked at Jamie, she might be tempted to blurt out everything that she and the team's PR rep had discussed that morning. The fallout, however, was not something she particularly wanted to deal with on team time. The longer she kept her online stalker situation from Jamie, the worse the outcome would be, but right now Jamie was playing well and seemed happy, and Emma didn't want to jeopardize that. The coaches would name the official World Cup roster in April. Jamie deserved to have the next couple of months go as smoothly and un-angstily as possible.

After Jo named the roster, Emma promised herself. She would tell Jamie everything then.

"She said a lot, actually," Emma admitted, watching as MSU's point guard stroked home a three. "I told her the social media contract requirement has been stressing me out, so she suggested I reduce my online footprint and focus on one platform. She also thinks I should hire one of the vendors on the federation's approved list to manage my social media presence."

She would probably end up keeping Twitter. Caroline had recommended withdrawing slowly from Facebook and Instagram so that she didn't provoke a corresponding "nuclear" response from any unstable fans. Emma had shuddered at the thought, and Caroline had reached across the conference table in the business suite at the National Training Center to pat her hand and assure her it wouldn't get to that.

But she couldn't really promise that. No one knew what a stalker was capable of until it was too late.

Jamie sat up beside her. "Wait. You're going to pay someone to run your official social media accounts for you?"

Emma could feel Jamie's gaze boring into the side of her face. "Well, yeah. I really want to focus on my game, and trying to remember what to post when is distracting. We didn't all grow up in Silicon Valley, you know."

"Berkeley is like an hour from Silicon Valley."

"You know what I mean," Emma said, and elbowed her lightly.

"You don't seem to have any problems with your private accounts."

"That's different." And it was. On her private Instagram and Facebook accounts, she could control who could see what, which was why she had never once experienced any sort of harassment on either platform. But

Twitter was a social media free-for-all, in more ways than one. "Mary Kate said it might be helpful to withdraw from my public accounts, too. Reducing online presence is helpful for people who are experiencing anxiety, which I definitely am at the moment."

At the mention of the team's sports psychologist, Jamie leaned back against the pillows. "Oh. Well, if Mary Kate thinks it's a good idea, you should definitely listen to her." She paused. "Would you maybe want me to run your public accounts? That is what I used to do for the guys at Arsenal. For free, though, obviously," she added. "I wouldn't mind helping out."

"No," Emma said, probably too quickly. She glanced at Jamie and squeezed her hand. "That's really sweet of you, but I think I'll have one of the vendors do it. I don't really want to waste any of our time together talking about sponsorships and tweet impressions. Okay?"

Jamie nodded, brow slightly furrowed. "Okay. So was that it? She didn't mention anything else?"

Emma hesitated. Caroline had, in fact, had quite a bit else to say. Namely, that Emma needed to collect a dossier on her would-be stalker. Screen shots, dates and times, proof that she'd reported violent or threatening messages to the social media powers that be—basically anything connected to her interaction with the guy needed to be documented. That way if law enforcement ever got involved, there would be a trail of evidence.

"She did mention we might want to keep our relationship quiet on social media," Emma said.

Jamie recoiled slightly. "Why? Because US Soccer would rather not acknowledge the queerness of this team's players or our fan base?"

"No," Emma said, "it's not like that." At least, she

didn't think it was. Caroline had said that displaying personal photos could be like waving a cape in front of a bull, which made sense to Emma. She didn't want to risk taking any action that might trigger the unstable man who seemed to be fixating on her.

Jamie pulled her hand from under Emma's and folded her arms across her chest. "Really? Then tell me: What is it like?"

Emma stared at her, wishing she could redo this sensitive conversation at a time when she wasn't exhausted from double training sessions and video reviews and virtual reality training and more fitness sessions than she could ever remember in her life. Not to mention when she'd had better sleep. At least she wasn't rooming with Britt. That girl's snoring could be heard two rooms away.

"It's more about keeping a low profile, that's all," she said, trying for a placating tone. "She and Mary Kate both said that if I was worrying about being distracted, I should probably keep my official accounts professional and leave the personal posts to my private pages."

This time, invoking the team psychologist's name didn't produce the same mollifying effect. Jamie's forehead remained furrowed as she demanded, "And you don't see any other possible motivating factor for a US Soccer rep to recommend that, Emma?"

Of course she did. But she'd decided not to fill Jamie in on the details of the situation until April, and she was damn well going to stick to that self-imposed deadline. "It's different for you, Jamie" she said. "You're publicly out."

"And you're not. I am well aware of that fact."

At the bitterness in her tone, Emma leaned away, putting space between them. "Do you have a problem with me not announcing my sexuality to the entire world? Because I have never lied to anyone about who I am."

"I know that, and it's totally your decision. But you could help so many kids, Emma. Can you imagine how many girls like you—and boys, for that matter—are out there right now hiding who they are and hating themselves for being different?"

"There are other bi and pansexual role models, you know," Emma pointed out. "Evan Rachael Wood, for one."

"Yes, and Michelle Rodriguez," Jamie said, waving a hand. "But there aren't any current athletes. At least, no one with your profile."

"I don't think Greta would appreciate hearing you say that." Greta Nilsson was the Swedish national team goalkeeper—and Jamie's teammate on the Portland Thorns.

Jamie rolled her eyes. "I meant American athletes. You could do so much good. We both could."

Emma couldn't believe that her conversation with the team's PR rep had turned into a referendum on whether or not she should out herself—and, by extension, their relationship—to the world. And yet, here they were.

She turned to face her girlfriend more fully. "There's a reason athletes don't come out, Jamie. Actors aren't available to the public the way we are. They work on closed sets with security, but we announce months in advance that we'll be in a certain place at a certain time. You know as well as I do that safety has been an issue since Monica Seles was stabbed in the '90s."

"But that's just it," Jamie argued. "None of us is ever fully safe. That's why I don't understand your obsession with privacy. We're already public figures."

Obsession? It was hardly that. Emma shook her head. "That's easy for you to say. Not only are you the heart on the sleeve type of person, you're like a thousand percent gay. You couldn't hide who you are even if you wanted to."

"And that's somehow easier? Because in case you wondered, it isn't easy being called a dyke for most of your life."

"I didn't say that part was easier. I just meant that I get why you don't understand my privacy thing because you don't have to deal with male fans the way I do."

"No kidding, Emma. The guys in the crowd either call me names or ignore me. Meanwhile, they're shirtless with your name spelled out on their bodies."

"Exactly. They write my name on their bodies. And why is that? Because they think I'm such an amazing soccer player? No, Jamie, it's because that's what I am to them: a body on display. If they knew I slept with women, my Twitter feed would be a hundred times worse than it already is." She stopped, because she hadn't meant to mention her problematic Twitter feed.

"I know, because they would think they had a shot at a threesome with you and some hot girl," Jamie said, sounding resigned. "Which, as we know, is every straight man's fantasy."

"Pretty much." She hesitated. Once again she was approaching territory she would rather not go into. "You may not know this, but Maddie had a stalker a couple of years ago. Not a game or open practice went by that she didn't worry about that guy appearing with a weapon. All she could think about, she told me, was that some little girl in the stands might get hurt because Maddie had somehow attracted this legitimately insane person."

That was the same fear that Emma lived with now, the

same horrible fantasy that flickered before her eyes before she left the tunnel at most of their US-based friendlies. The idea that *she* could be the reason someone else—Jamie, a little girl in the crowd, a soccer mom or dad—got hurt was almost unbearable at times, especially late at night when worry maintained its stubborn grip on her subconscious.

"I didn't know that." Jamie reached for Emma's hand again. "But she didn't attract him, Em. He fixated on her. That's different."

"Maybe in theory, but not in practice." The TV crowd erupted, and Emma used the sound as an excuse to turn away from the empathy in Jamie's eyes. It would be so easy to unburden herself, so much better to execute Operation Reduce Social Media Presence with Jamie firmly on her side. But she had involved Sam the last time, and their relationship had ended soon after. She wasn't about to risk what she and Jamie had together now.

April, she reminded herself. There would be plenty of time to deal with everything then. Besides, hadn't Jamie once said Emma didn't owe her details about her past? The present was a different matter, but they would figure it out together. Eventually.

Sighing, she rested her head on Jamie's shoulder. "Can we be done with this conversation? Is that okay? I'm tired, and it's almost curfew."

Beside her, Jamie shifted closer again. "Of course."

They were quiet for a little while, Emma watching the TV screen but not really taking in the blur of moving athletes or the streak of partisan colors. Was she doing the right thing in keeping difficult truths from Jamie? Was there any way to know for sure? Probably not until well after everything shook out. Possibly not even then.

"I can hear you thinking," Jamie said softly, pressing a

kiss into her hair.

"I know," Emma said, but she didn't elaborate.

"I don't want you to think I don't respect your decisions. You're right, I don't know what it's like to be you any more than you know what it's like to be me. But I'd like to understand."

She was so sweet and open, and Emma would never, she was pretty sure, be good enough for her. When they were teenagers, Jamie had used her assault as motivation to improve herself while Emma had basically run from her father's death. Instead of processing her grief, she'd sprinted toward her future goals: a national championship with UNC, a permanent spot on the national team, a gold medal at the Olympics, and now another chance at gold at the World Cup. And yes, she had done some work on herself in the intervening years, but she couldn't deny the feeling that Jamie was better at managing the external pressures on their relationship.

Before she could respond, the door's electronic lock beeped. Reluctantly, Emma moved away from Jamie. By the time Gabe appeared at the foot of the bed, they were seated side by side with a respectable gap between them—like the romantically uninvolved teammates they definitely were not.

"Hey, guys," Gabe said, and flopped down on the other bed. "How goes it?"

"I'm so tired," Jamie admitted, laughing a little. "I don't think I've ever run so many intervals in my life."

"Right?" Emma agreed, relieved to think about something other than her pathetic emotional skills.

"To be fair, Lacey did warn us ahead of time," Gabe pointed out. As an outside midfielder, she routinely placed at the top of the charts in any competition that involved endurance.

"Yeah, but I didn't realize how serious she was," Emma said.

"Same." Jamie smiled at her, and Emma smiled back.

They would be okay, she told herself, trying one of the deep breaths Mary Kate had suggested she learn to cultivate. Apparently research showed that deep breathing calmed the mind, even if researchers weren't entirely sure why. Maybe Emma would even learn to meditate. Jamie swore by it, and MK had assured her that the practice offered many promising returns for elite athletes. For now, though, Emma was satisfied exploring the new visualization exercises MK had offered.

The basketball game continued on in the background as they chatted with Gabe for a little while longer, the white noise of the cheering crowd familiar and somehow comforting as they gossiped about teammates and discussed families and friends they shared in common. Then Gabe collected her things and disappeared into the bathroom for a shower, leaving them alone again.

"Guess I should say goodnight," Jamie said, snuggling back into her side.

"Guess so," Emma agreed. But even so, she tightened her grip on Jamie's hand. "I wish you could stay."

"I know. Think Gabe might want to trade rooms for the night?"

"Um, I think people might notice."

"You're probably right." Jamie sighed audibly.

Emma nudged her shoulder. "Don't worry. We'll be home soon."

"Home, huh," Jamie echoed, giving her a definite side-eye.

"You know what I mean. The Pacific Northwest."

"Right." Jamie was still watching her. "Feel like company up there in Seattle?"

"Of course. Feel like staying with me?"

"I would love it."

"Good," Emma said, "because I love you."

"I love you too," Jamie replied, her smile unabashedly sentimental.

"Awesome."

"Excellent."

Emma leaned in and kissed her, slow and soft, but even the light pressure of Jamie's lips against hers made her body vibrate with restless energy. It was just as difficult as ever to be around Jamie so much without being able to really be with her except for brief, rushed encounters. At that moment, Emma couldn't wait to get back to Seattle, where they would have nearly a week together before they flew to France. Or, until *she* flew to Europe, anyway. Jamie's presence on the national team roster was still a camp-by-camp, match-by-match affair.

The water shut off in the bathroom—Gabe was legendary for taking the fastest showers of anyone on the team—and Emma pulled back, resting her forehead against Jamie's. "Let's hunker down in my apartment when we get back and not go anywhere."

"Hunker down?" Jamie repeated, laughing.

"I'm serious. Nowhere at all for at least forty-eight hours."

"Count me in," Jamie said, and kissed the tip of her nose. Then she slipped from the bed, pausing to stretch her arms over her head and make the sweet puppy squeak Emma had always loved. "See you at breakfast?"

"Absolutely."

Emma didn't walk her out tonight, simply waved and watched as Jamie ducked out of the room before returning her attention to the game. The teams seemed well matched. Out of loyalty to her mother's Midwestern roots, she decided to cheer for MSU. With the Penn State sex abuse scandal not all that far in the past, she found it difficult to imagine cheering for that particular athletic program ever again. Jamie's dad, Emma knew, took an even more extreme view and insisted that Penn State football should have been permanently banned from NCAA competition.

Tim, Jamie's dad, was a good person. Emma wished he could have met her father. She also wished that Sarah, Jamie's mother, had met Emma's dad more than that one, emotionally fraught time. The familiar bittersweet ache at the thought of what could have been rose inside her, and Emma hugged her knees to her chest. She doubted the feeling would ever go away entirely, which wasn't a bad thing. She would never fully forget her father, not until she was old and gray and had begun to lose herself the way her grandmother had before she'd died—assuming concussions didn't get her memory first.

Gabe came out of the bathroom already dressed in the boxer shorts and T-shirt she wore as pajamas, her long brown hair curling damp around her shoulders. Originally from Colorado, she had played in college at University of Portland and now played professionally with Emma for the Reign. In the off-season, though, she went back to Denver where most of her family still resided.

"Did Jamie take off?" Gabe asked.

"Yeah. Unfortunately."

"How are you two doing? I know it isn't easy to manage a relationship like this." As she arranged herself on the other bed, Gabe waved her hand, the gesture presumably encompassing the hotel, the National Training Center, and Carson beyond.

"We're actually doing okay." Emma hesitated. "But… can I ask you something?"

Gabe glanced over at her. "Sure."

"Have you ever had any problems with social media? Like threats or anything?"

"No, I haven't. But Ellie has, and so has Maddie. Jenny, too, I think. Why? Is it happening to you and Jamie?"

"A little." The list Gabe had provided matched the one Emma had compiled in her head after Caroline had told her she wasn't the only team member struggling with this issue. *Christ.* Wouldn't it be awesome if men didn't act like assholes online? Then again, plenty of them were assholes in real life. Why would they behave any differently in a virtual space where they could be anonymous?

"I'm sorry," Gabe said, giving her a sympathetic grimace. "Is there anything I can do?"

"No. But thanks."

"Of course. My apartment in Seattle is yours if you guys ever need it."

"Thanks," she said, touched by the offer. "I hope we don't, though."

"I hope not, either," Gabe agreed.

They turned off the lights a little while later and Emma lay in bed like she had been doing lately, listening to her heartbeat race as the near-nightly anxiety swept over her. She still couldn't believe she'd managed to lose her starting spot. Would *she* even make the roster for Europe? What about the Algarve Cup? Her contract renewal was scheduled for some time this spring. What if the federation decided not to renew her? What if she got cut in a World Cup year? And even if she didn't, what if the stalker came after her in real life? Worse, what if he came after Jamie?

For fuck's sake, she thought, trying to breathe deeply through the onslaught of irrational fears. Why couldn't her mind just shut the hell up? But it didn't, and so she lay there with her ear plugs in and her eyeshade on, fighting her brain's unnecessary injection of adrenaline into her system. She wished she were home in Seattle with Jamie curled up beside her under the covers, her touch leeching peace and calm into Emma's body as surely as the constellations shifted overhead in the night sky.

Soon, she told herself, picturing her quiet building, her multiple deadbolts, her comfortable apartment. *Soon.*

CHAPTER THREE

"Seriously, it's starting to feel like we're never going to play again," Ryan Dierdorf muttered as she took her place at one end of the thick battle ropes Lacey had brought along to France to torture them with.

Jamie managed to contain her eye roll as she picked up the ropes next to Ryan's. They were staying at a five-star hotel on the Quiberon Peninsula in Brittany that sported ocean views, impressive fitness facilities, and an on-site spa. Right this very minute, they were training on a sunny hotel terrace mere steps from the heated pool where Jamie planned to relax again after dinner. A few paces in the other direction lay sandy beaches and the Atlantic Ocean, close enough to practically feel drops of spray carried on the wind. For the veterans, this might be same old, same old, but Jamie felt incredibly lucky to be here. Still, entitled players were going to gripe. In Jamie's experience, once someone felt secure in their position on a team, it was basically human nature to complain.

After their three-week camp at the National Training Center, most of the team had arrived in France chomping at the bit to compete with someone (*anyone*) other than each other. Jo's continued willingness to give Lacey Rodriguez the reins for what even Ellie, an apparently huge Jo Nichols fan, had conceded felt like overkill on the fitness front was not helping. Jamie was a morning person, and even she was finding it more and more difficult to peel herself out of bed for their daily morning fitness session.

At least afternoon training sessions took place on an actual soccer field. The field in question—a local stadium not far from the hotel—reminded Jamie of various UK pitches where she had played with Arsenal. With only 3,000 seats, it was a far cry from the American stadiums the other players were used to. But the surface was synthetic, just like the game field where they were scheduled to play France in a few days, and the town itself was quiet and out-of-the-way. Even in the summer, they'd been told, the Quiberon Peninsula typically attracted local French tourists. In the first week of February, there didn't seem to be many of those.

"Come on, James," Angie called from the other side of the terrace. She tugged on her end of the battle ropes, nearly upending Jamie. "Bring it!"

"Oh, it has already been broughten!" Jamie hollered back. When Lacey's assistant blew her whistle, they each started moving the ropes up and down rhythmically, creating opposing waves that met in the middle. Their turn lasted a full minute. By the time the whistle blew again, Jamie's arm muscles were burning nicely.

After catching her breath, she met Angie at the side of the terrace for the next station: push-ups for a minute. The final station of the morning was throwing a medicine ball back and forth for—*yep*—another minute. This was their third and final time through the terrace stations. After this, they would be free for a couple of hours before lunch.

"Take that," Angie said, pushing the medicine ball at

her chest.

Jamie caught it easily. "You can do better than that, short stuff."

"Did you honestly just call me short stuff?"

"Why, do you have a problem with reality?"

They kept up the banter until the final whistle blew, and then they flopped down on the grass beside each other, stretching their tired muscles. The previous station had involved side planks, seated crunches on a yoga ball, and reverse crunches. Before that they'd done a circuit of the hotel's weight room, preceded by 45 minutes of cardio. Some people had opted for a run around the peninsula, which was only nine miles long and on average a mile and a half wide. Jamie and Angie, however, had opted for laps in the hotel's indoor pool that boasted wide windows overlooking the beach.

"Too bad you couldn't keep up," Angie said now, clucking disapprovingly as she stretched out her hamstrings.

"As if."

"Go on, laugh it up. We'll see who starts on Sunday."

"Hate to tell you, Ange, but it isn't going to be either of us."

"Probably not. But at least we'll always have Quiberon."

Like everyone else on the team, she pronounced the peninsula's name with suitable drama and an extra dollop of friction on the *r*, just like the locals. Well, maybe not just like the locals. But close.

Once they were stretched, they headed indoors to get cleaned up and take a nap before lunch. Jamie knocked on Emma's door, but she didn't answer, so Jamie continued on to her own room. Probably Emma was still finishing up her fitness rotation. They'd been in different groups yet again. Angie and Maddie had noticed it too—right from the start of January camp, the coaches had begun dividing the team into groups that nearly always split the two couples. Angie and Maddie had called the imposed separation overkill, but Emma and Jamie had agreed privately that it wasn't a big deal. As long as the federation didn't try to tell them they couldn't be a couple, they didn't mind being separated at practice.

Then again, Jamie thought as she scrubbed the smell of chlorine from her skin with the hotel's French lavender body scrub, hadn't the federation basically told them not to be a couple publicly? Caroline, the team's PR rep, had recently counseled Emma to keep their relationship quiet. What had Emma called it? Oh, right: *Keeping a low profile.* She could call it whatever she wanted, but what it boiled down to was that US Soccer wanted them to stay in the closet. Even Jamie's non-rostered player contract, required for participation in training and friendlies, had a relationship clause.

For now, she would play their game. Once she earned a positon on the permanent roster, then she would set her closet door on fire, just as Ellie had done before her. Playing politics was one of many skills that elite athletes had to master. Or, you know, at least not *flounder* at. No one would ever accuse Jamie of being particularly shrewd, but she liked to think that she'd gained a modicum of sophistication over the years. She would never be at Emma's or Ellie's level, but that was fine. That's what she kept them around for.

Why they kept her around, she still hadn't quite figured out.

Her lack of political finesse was probably how, the

following night, she found herself on a team of non-bowlers. Normally, this wouldn't present a problem, but given they were currently at a bowling alley with the rest of the team, the situation was not ideal. The outing was a surprise, tacked on at the end of a planned practice at Stade du Moustoir, the stadium in Lorient where they would face France at the end of the week. The players had thought they were merely stopping at a seafood restaurant on the way back to the hotel, but after dining on fresh local catch, they'd filed back onto the bus only to gaze at each other in bemusement when the charter bus pulled up at a low-slung building that looked like a business park—except for the fluorescent "Bowling" marquee.

Jo rose at the front of the bus and held up a hand to stop the tide of murmurs. "We thought you might appreciate getting out of the hotel tonight and doing something fun."

"And competitive, of course," Melanie Beckett, the defensive coach, added. "The winning team gets to sleep in tomorrow."

A cheer went up through the chartered coach, and Jamie grinned before she remembered: Bowling was not a skill she had ever cultivated.

"Don't look at me," Lisa said once the teams had been divvied up. "Bowling is one of the whitest sports on Earth."

Jamie glanced at Jordan and Rebecca, who were laughing at each other's rented shoes. "What about you guys? VB, didn't you live in Arizona for a while?"

Jordan shot her a quizzical look. "Yeah, but Tucson isn't exactly known for its bowling scene."

"So none of us know what we're doing?" Jamie lamented.

"It could still be fun," Rebecca tried.

"If you don't mind losing," Lisa said.

They exchanged weighted glances. As if that could really be a thing.

Mentally preparing for the worst, Jamie went to find a bowling ball. She was lucky to be here, she reminded herself. *L-U-C-K-Y.*

Despite the fact they came in dead last, Jamie and her mates on Team "I Can't Believe It's Not Gutter" (ironically named, given that they threw more gutters than anyone in the history of bowling) did end up having a good time. They were with friends, and they were inside a warm, dry establishment rather than outdoors freezing their butts off in the cold wind off the Atlantic. Part of Jamie's enjoyment involved watching Emma's approach, her hips swinging in her low-slung jeans, her eyes deadly serious as she took aim at the white pins arranged at the end of her lane. The exaggerated flourish at the end of her delivery would have been almost embarrassing if she didn't throw strike after strike. Her perfect bowling form derived from her years at UNC, Jamie knew, as did her similarly noteworthy skills in beer pong, darts, pool, and quarters.

Team "Bowling Stones" took top honors, a fact that Emma and Angie made sure to rub in during the hour-plus ride back to the hotel, engaging in the usual shit-talking while the rest of the team acted like they couldn't care less who had won. But they cared, Jamie knew. Every last one of them. Even Rebecca.

"How did you get so good at bowling, anyway?" Maddie asked Angie at one point, presumably to distract her from the annoying bragging.

"Are you kidding? There's nothing to do in Jersey except bowl."

A description that Jamie was pretty sure also fit North Carolina's Research Triangle region.

The bus let them off at the hotel's main entrance. Jamie followed her teammates across the beautiful lobby with its cozy fire and murals of Celtic dragons, heading for the corridor that led to the team's room block. The majority of their rooms had two single beds, though a few players had to share rooms with one king. Since bed sharing was involved, the coaches had taken more input than they usually did in roommate assignments. They couldn't exactly force Jamie, for example, to share a king room with a homophobe like Jessica North.

As a result, Maddie and Emma had ended up in a two-single room while Jamie and Angie had volunteered to take a king, and then had proceeded to spend most evenings before curfew with their girlfriends in one or the other room. One night, Jamie had gone for a walk with Lisa, Gabe, and Rebecca, and when she came back, Angie wasn't in their room. In fact, Jamie was pretty sure she hadn't returned until the wee hours of the morning. When she'd asked Emma about it later, Emma told her that Angie and Maddie had fallen asleep together in Maddie's twin bed, exhausted from the never-ending double sessions.

Which was sweet and all, but the thought of breaking the federation's rules so blatantly creeped Jamie out. She couldn't imagine taking that kind of risk with her still-nascent national team career, inadvertently or not.

She was almost to the stairwell when she felt a hand on her arm. Emma.

Her girlfriend nodded to a door that led to the main terrace. "Do you want to build a snowman?" she asked, her eyebrows waggling.

Jamie burst out laughing as she stepped out of the stream of players crowding into the stairwell. "Seeing as there's currently no snow…"

"Want to take a walk out to the point, then? The moonrise looked pretty amazing, and curfew's still an hour away."

"Um." The answer was *yes*, of course she wanted to go for a moonlit walk with her gorgeous girlfriend at whom she had been gazing longingly for the past couple of hours. But at the same time, it was freaking cold here at night. The Atlantic Ocean didn't mess around.

"We can borrow winter coats from the front desk," Emma offered.

"How do you know that?"

"I asked. You don't get what—"

"—you don't ask for," Jamie said, finishing Emma's father's motto. "Yes, I know. It just never would have occurred to me to ask for something like that."

Emma smiled and, kindly, didn't point out the disparity in their incomes and world-traveling experiences.

"If there are winter coats involved, then I'm in," Jamie decided.

"Awesome." Emma started to reach for her hand, but bit her lip instead and turned away. "Follow me."

Five minutes later, they were bundled into white ski jackets with faux fur-lined hoods—at least, Jamie hoped it was faux fur. They headed down the footpath that led to a promontory 50 yards from the hotel, picking their way carefully over the rocky shore. The path was semi-lit by garden lights and a fair amount of moonlight, but Emma turned on her phone's flashlight anyway. Neither of them could afford to twist an ankle or knee on an after-hours stroll.

As they walked, Jamie slipped her arm through

Emma's and pulled her closer. They were well outside the reach of the hotel's lights, and while they might not be the only people out here, she doubted the coaches were around. Even if they were, Jamie could blame the cold. She wouldn't even be lying.

Overhead, the moon rose bright and nearly full. At the end of the trail sat a bench with the hotel's logo. They dropped onto it, and Emma shut off her flashlight and snuggled in against Jamie's side, their arms still looped. It almost reminded Jamie of—

"It's a little colder than Del Mar, isn't it?" Emma commented.

"That's exactly what I was thinking," Jamie said, smiling at her in the moonlight while white-crested waves crashed against the nearby Breton rocks.

They sat quietly for a few minutes, huddled together in their borrowed hotel couture, the tide shifting farther out to sea with every passing moment. Then Jamie asked, "Do you ever wonder what would have happened if we'd never taken that walk?"

"Sometimes," Emma said, her eyes dark in the shadows cast by the moon. "But I still think we would have ended up here. Don't you?"

"I don't know," Jamie admitted. "You were there for me at a really crucial time, Emma. I'm not sure I'd be here if it wasn't for you."

"Do you mean *here*, like in France with the national team? Or…?"

"Both," she confessed. It was easier to be honest with Emma's eyes focused on the crashing waves, the white surf glowing in the moonlight. "Your father wasn't wrong. I was a mess when you met me."

Emma hesitated before asking, "Did you ever think of

ending everything?"

Jamie swallowed and said honestly, "I think so. The time right after the trip is a little blurry now, so I don't really remember. I just know I wanted it all to go away. I felt like I couldn't stay in my skin anymore." She shivered, remembering the despair that had filled her with heaviness, the fear that had lurked just below the surface, ready to seize control of her brain at any given moment.

Emma found her hand in her jacket pocket and squeezed, her touch reassuring.

"I don't think I would have actually done anything," Jamie told her, not because she knew for a fact that this was true but because she wanted it to be. "I had a really hard time sleeping afterward, and I think that made me a little crazy. When you and I met, I couldn't fall sleep without smoking up. Even then, half the time I would wake up from this nightmare that was basically my brain replaying what had happened, over and over." She shook her head. "For the longest time, I was convinced I would never be totally free of that dream."

"And now?" Emma asked, her voice careful.

"I haven't had one in years." The realization made Jamie sit up straighter, the burden she carried—the one she would always carry—suddenly a bit lighter.

"Good." Emma paused again, and then she said, "You know, I might not be here either—with the national team, I mean—if it weren't for you."

Jamie frowned slightly. "What are you talking about?"

"Without you, I might have gone even more off the rails than I did when my dad died."

"You did kind of go off the rails. I mean, come on, Tori Parker?"

Emma huffed out a laugh. "Yes, I've heard once or twice that she and I were not the best idea. No one has said anything like that about you, though."

"Yeah?" Jamie smiled over at her.

"Yeah." Emma touched a cold hand to her cheek. "I think I see why."

"Oh, you think, do you—?" Jamie started to tease her, but then Emma's lips were on hers, and she willingly gave up speaking.

"Let's come back here someday on a real vacation," she whispered a little while later. "Just the two of us."

"I would love to." Emma smiled up at her, eyes and teeth glowing in the moonlight. "But maybe when it's a little warmer."

"Absolutely."

She imagined it: long nights together between high thread-count sheets, sunny days swimming in the hotel's private cove, evenings dining on the patio near the ocean because it would be warm enough to have dinner outside the next time they visited. Or the heat lamps on the hotel's patio would make it so, anyway. She wasn't convinced Brittany was ever all that warm.

They stayed on the bench until just before curfew, and then they went back to their separate rooms, reluctantly saying goodnight in the hallway as their teammates returned from the hot tub and the pool and wherever else they had gone to kill the final hour of the day. Then Jamie returned to her and Angie's room, where she took a long shower, waiting for the hot spray to warm her frozen legs all the way through.

It took a while. Then again, her showers almost always did.

Angie was already in bed with the bedside lamp off when Jamie emerged from their bathroom. Apparently it was exhausting to win a fake bowling tournament.

"Emma texted you," the diminutive midfielder said, not bothering to remove her sleep mask.

"How did you…?" Jamie started to ask, but then she realized that the notification she'd chosen for Emma's calls and texts was easily recognizable: a crowd erupting in cheers. "I mean, thanks."

"Welcome. Please note that I am blindfolded and have ear plugs in."

Was Angie saying she and Emma could have phone sex? Or even Skype sex? Because, *ew*.

"Meaning," Angie added, "that if you were to vanish from this room, I wouldn't know. Plausible deniability, bud."

"Got it," Jamie said, even as she grimaced at the memory of the last time she'd snuck out of a French hotel. Besides, Emma would never go for such a thing. Would she?

Jamie grabbed her phone and checked her messages. Emma had texted a picture of her bed and added the caption, "Wish you were here… XOXO"

She hesitated for a moment before typing, "Miss you too. Goodnight! XOXO."

Emma's reply came back a moment later: "Sweet dreams."

"Sweet dreams to you too."

This was the right decision, Jamie told herself as she turned off her phone. Team rules existed for a reason, and even if they didn't, that didn't make them any less real. Angie, Maddie, and Emma had contracts that couldn't easily be scrapped. If they were caught breaking the rules, their consequences would be more along the lines of a reprimand. Even Jenny Latham, who had once gotten caught skinny-dipping drunk at a team hotel—with a random dude, no less—had only been suspended for a couple of months. Jamie, on the other hand, was operating on a temporary agreement that made it easier for the federation to terminate her than to promote her to the full roster.

She had made the right decision, she assured herself again, stretching out on her bed with her iPad tuned to Archive of Our Own. There would be other trips with romantic moonlit walks where it was just her and Emma, with no one from US Soccer within a thousand-mile radius. They would have plenty of time in the future to be themselves together—she hoped.

#

A few days later, Jamie gazed out the window as the bus sped along the two-lane road that connected the Quiberon Peninsula to the main coast of Brittany. Currently they were headed to Lorient for their friendly against France. After the game, they would catch a charter flight to London, where they would train for a few days before the second match against England on the 13th. Valentine's Day would see them back on a plane, headed home after nearly two weeks in Europe.

At least she and Emma would be spending V-Day together this time, even if they would be traveling halfway—a quarter of the way?—across the planet that day. They wouldn't have much time at home before the Algarve Cup started, though, assuming they both made the roster for Portugal. All of this ping-ponging back and forth from Europe to the US was difficult, and for most people would only end when NWSL preseason started. Not for

Jamie, though—Arsenal was set to meet Paris-St. Germain (PSG) in the Champions League quarterfinals in late March, and if they won those two matches, they would play Lyon in the semis in April.

Lyon, where Jamie had managed not to set foot since before she and Emma had met.

As the bus crossed the sandy isthmus that connected Quiberon to the mainland, Jamie said a silent goodbye to the small peninsula. Surprisingly, she had been sorry to check out of the hotel that afternoon. The handful of other times she'd returned to France—for national youth team tournaments, for Champions League her first year at Arsenal, for vacation once with Clare—she had gritted her teeth and braved the waves of reaction to being in the same country where her assault had taken place more than a decade ago. But this time, maybe because she was working to make the World Cup squad or maybe because she was older and, one would hope, wiser, or maybe simply because Emma had been at her side throughout the trip, the waves of fear had felt smaller, more manageable. Not once had she felt herself sliding into the black hole of past emotional trauma.

It helped that Brittany and the Rhône-Alpes region shared little in common. Lyon was one of the largest cities in France with a population of more than two million, while Quiberon's population topped out around five thousand. The quaint peninsula reminded Jamie of a beach town along the central Oregon Coast, only centuries older, of course. Lyon, on the other hand, was a two thousand year old urban center that featured a mix of Roman, Renaissance, and modern architecture, with rivers and hills rather than sandy beaches and rocky coves. Both regions were beautiful, but to Jamie, they almost seemed like entirely different nations.

On past visits to France, Jamie had spent most of her time either on a football field or playing tourist in the nation's better-known cities. For this trip, however, the coaching staff had made good use of their week on the coast. Two mornings ago, their fitness session had consisted of a guided kayak tour along the "Wild Coast" of Quiberon, while yesterday they'd gone for a group run—five miles along quiet country lanes overlooking the ocean to Pointe du Percho, where they poked around sand dunes and sandy coves at low tide. Ellie had even talked Jamie into joining her for a sunrise swim this morning, one of her Game Day traditions (where available). Although "swim" was an exaggeration. In reality, they had walked into the water, submerged their bodies for all of 20 seconds—possibly less—before squealing and hightailing it back to the nearby heated pool. Still, the cold water had been refreshing, much like one of the ice baths Ellie and Emma swore by.

But now Game Day was in full swing. Kickoff was a bit early—six p.m., which meant they'd eaten the day's meals early, including "dinner" at three before boarding the bus to the stadium. Jamie hoped there would be food served on the flight to London. Otherwise there would be a whole lot of hangry women traveling in close quarters today. They damn well better beat France, too, or heads would roll.

She giggled to herself at the guillotine reference and then schooled her features back into a stoic mask as Emma glanced at her. Probably better to keep her nerd humor to herself on Game Day.

#

The crowd was difficult, she realized immediately. The dark-clad fans whistled at the officials and at the American players with little provocation, their shouts and singing dominated by male voices—so unlike the family-friendly crowds Jamie had grown accustomed to back home. The weather was cold and clear, and the pitch was fast. Artificial turf was always speedy even when the groundskeepers didn't water the surface before a game like they had today. The French team, comfortable on their home field in front of a crowd of fifteen thousand, had come out ready to play. The US, on the other hand, started on their heels. But they soon recovered and went on the attack, narrowly missing two scoring opportunities near the end of the first half.

With the score stuck at 0-0 at halftime, Jo's locker room talk wasn't exactly sunshine and rainbows, but it was generally positive. There were 45 minutes left, she reminded them, and they had several good things to take from the first half—ball movement, technical touches, and passing in the offensive third—and build on in the second. Despite the hostile crowd, the coaches were confident that the US was in control of the game.

Sometimes the two halves of a soccer game could seem like entirely different matches. Momentum could shift on a blown call or a quick counterattack, and all at once, the team that had been controlling play found themselves scrambling to catch up. That was what the second half against France felt like, Jamie thought. Only five minutes in and Lindsay Martens, a newbie player starting at outside defender in place of an injured Emily Shorter, had somehow allowed her player to not only score the first goal of the game but assist on the second. Jo and Melanie didn't wait for her to recover her shaken poise. They yanked her and moved Taylor O'Brien from the center to outside back, which meant they needed another central defender to take Taylor's spot. They needed Emma.

Sure enough, Jo glanced down the bench and barked

Emma's name. Jamie caught her girlfriend's eye and gave her a thumbs-up. *You can do this.* Emma nodded back subtly and checked in with the fourth official, jumping up and down as Martens jogged off the field, her head bowed. Jamie felt bad for the kid. A standout for Kansas City in the NWSL and a recent winner of the collegiate MAC Hermann Trophy award, Lindsay had been floating around the pool for the past year. When Shorter sprained her knee at the end of January camp, Lindsay had made her first friendly roster. Now what had been a literal dream come true was turning into a nightmare.

Emma slapped hands with Martens and murmured something no doubt supportive before running onto the field, her body language the opposite of the pulled defender's. In the aftermath of the Brazil trip, Emma's confidence had been MIA. But slowly, over the course of January camp and in training here in Brittany, she had seemed to come back to herself. Now as she took the field, Jamie thought she could see the old Emma, moving with purpose and a sense of coiled energy waiting to burst into action.

She hadn't been in for long when Jo looked down the bench again and said, "Ellie, Maxwell, warm up."

And just like that, Jamie forgot to worry about Emma. She joined the team captain on the sideline, keeping one eye on the game as they went through the familiar warm-up exercises.

"You got this," Ellie said, bumping her fist when Jo motioned to them again.

God, Jamie hoped so.

Steph came off at the next dead ball, jogging over to the sideline to slap Jamie's hand and to tell her to "watch number 3," as they passed. Then Jamie was sprinting out onto the field and assuming her place in the middle just in front of Emma. Their eyes met and Emma nodded at her, her expression simultaneously fierce and confident, and Jamie's stomach flipped once before settling into place. She had this. She totally did.

The game she entered was nothing like the last time she'd played for the US side. Against Brazil, the game had been slower paced, more patient, neither side interested in taking too many risks. Brazil had only needed a tie to win their International Tournament of Nations, and after losing to them in the round robin, the US hadn't been eager to repeat that experience. But this game—this game was a mad scramble from the moment Jamie set foot on the turf. She knew a few of the French players from Champions League and the NWSL, but she was still surprised at how technical they were, how quickly they seized upon any mistake the American team made. The crowd was knowledgeable and passionate, and Jamie could sense the excitement infusing the stadium. France was number three in the world and headed to Canada in a few months as a legitimate contender to win the World Cup. Beating the US, Olympic champions and, until recently, the number one team in the world, would be a boon for the French. The Americans, on the other hand, were stuck in a desperate game of catch-up while struggling not to fall even farther behind. Not exactly the best combination.

Fifteen minutes after she entered, Jamie drove toward the French box, her defender scrambling in her wake. Maddie was up front and called for the ball, and Jamie sliced it to her on an angle. Then she made an overlapping run to the corner, putting on a burst of speed as Maddie slotted the ball back to her. She caught it just before it hit the end line and one-timed a pass to the twelve, where Ellie was waiting. Time seemed to slow as Ellie raised into the air, her form picture perfect, and struck the ball with her head. The crowd gasped and Jamie watched, holding her breath, as the ball arced toward the goal—and hit the crossbar. The French keeper fell on the rebound, and Ellie paused briefly, holding her hands to her head.

Damn it, Jamie thought as she jogged back on defense. So close. But at least they were getting chances. At least they were still in the game.

Time ticked away seemingly faster and faster, though, and as the half dwindled to a close, the American side failed to finish any of their chances. When the final whistle blew, the score was still 2-0. Jamie could hardly believe it. The French, only one step behind them in the international rankings, had actually shut them out.

The stands emptied quickly as the exultant French fans headed back out into the world, leaving the American side to gather their gear and hurry to the airport to catch their charter flight to England. As they pulled away from the stadium, Jamie could see the French flag flying proudly. She looked away, hoping it wouldn't be the flag that would fly above the winners' podium in Canada this summer. Because honestly, she already had enough shitty history with the nation of France.

CHAPTER FOUR

Emma nestled into her couch as she pulled up Super Bowl XLIX on her DVR. They had just gotten home from London that afternoon, and she was, frankly, amazed that she had somehow managed not to see the final score while traveling with the national team in Europe. It helped that Europeans were notoriously disinterested in American football, as the NFL was referred to outside of the US, and the rest of the team had been just as determined as she was not to see any spoilers. The few people who did know what happened were kind enough to preserve the mystery for those who didn't. That was part of the team's general ethos—you didn't mess around with sports.

"Ready?" she called to Jamie, who she could hear thumping around in the bedroom.

"Hold on," Jamie called back.

Emma tapped her foot against the coffee table, eyes on the view beyond her living room windows. The 12th man flag was flying atop the Space Needle as usual at this time of year, but that didn't necessarily mean Seattle had beaten the Patriots to win their second Super Bowl in a row. It only meant that the city of Seattle encouraged the rabidity of local fans to a potentially unhealthy degree—another thing Emma loved about her hometown.

Jamie emerged from the hall, looking adorable and comfortable in fleece sweats and one of Emma's many UNC soccer hoodies, water bottle and bag of Smartfood in hand. "Now I'm ready," she said, dropping down onto the couch and propping her feet on the coffee table beside Emma's. "Happy Valentine's Day."

"Happy Valentine's Day," Emma said, leaning in to kiss Jamie's smile. They had exchanged V-Day cards on the plane and were planning a romantic dinner out later in the week, but tonight they'd decided to make do with popcorn and Whole Foods sushi. As Jamie smiled at her and reached for her hand, Emma felt some of the tension seep from her nervous system. She hit play and leaned back, snuggling into Jamie's side. Thank god they were home—at least for a little while.

After a relaxing, productive week in Brittany, the team had suffered a long, rough trip across Northern Europe and back home again, with choppy air and weather-related travel delays compounded by losing to France and barely managing to defeat England. During the game in Milton Keynes, just north of London, the British team had had their game-tying goal called back on a questionable offsides penalty. If not for the referee's blunder, the US may well have finished their European tour 0-1-1.

Hardly an auspicious start to the year, if you asked Emma. But Jo and the other coaches claimed to be fine with the results because adversity helped build character and you never knew who you were until the chips were down, and so on and so forth. Still, it was sort of the wrong year to be experimenting with the lineup, wasn't it? Shouldn't they have their starting 11 mostly set at this point, only a few months out from Canada?

And it wasn't just that Emma had played less than half of the France match and not a single second against England. Jamie had sat the bench in her adopted home country too, which was, honestly, shitty. But whatever. Emma was doing better with being benched. She was doing better with accepting her role on the team as a non-starter and cheering her teammates on from the sideline. Or, at least, she was doing better putting on a positive face about her lack of playing time. What she actually wanted, of course, was to demand the opportunity to fight for her spot during a match, preferably a match that counted.

The Super Bowl was still in the first quarter when Jamie nudged her. "Hey."

"Yeah?" Emma asked, keeping her eyes on the television.

"You're secretly psyched about how the trip turned out, aren't you?"

"Total—wait," Emma said, her mind catching up belatedly. "What are you talking about?"

"I'm talking about the part where the team struggled to win without you on the field," Jamie clarified.

Of course Jamie would see through her fake smiles. "Maybe," Emma allowed.

"Good," Jamie said, and tossed a piece of cheddar-covered popcorn into her mouth. "Because I've waited long enough to play with the best defender in the world. Jo needs to not fuck this up for me."

If Emma's eyes pricked with tears, it was only because she was tired from the trip.

Later, after watching Seattle lose the Super Bowl on the goal line in the final minute by changing up their game rather than sticking with who—er, *what* had brought them that far, Emma lay in bed beside a softly snoring Jamie, unable to shake the worry that Seattle's loss was another bad omen. While Jo had claimed the team's struggles against quality European opponents were acceptable because the coaches wanted them to peak this summer, the players hadn't quite seen it that way. Nor had the women's soccer press. In the wake of the US loss at Lorient, the media had focused on the lack of cohesion among the back five and the disarray in the midfield, where the 4-4-2 system they were fielding clearly required at least one defensive-minded midfielder.

The problem, as even Jo had conceded, was that most of the midfielders on the team were 10s, which meant they were offensive-minded first and foremost. Under the current system, they'd tied and lost to Brazil in December, and now they'd lost to the number three team in the world and nearly tied sixth-ranked England. The Algarve Cup would be a referendum on the coaching staff, more than one commentator had noted. Many of the players agreed. During pre-match training in the UK, Emma had heard enough muttering about lineups and personnel that she couldn't help remembering the previous year's Algarve, when the team had finished an excruciating seventh.

This time, though, Ellie had their coach's back.

"Give Jo time," she'd counseled more than once on their tour of Northern Europe. "And in the meantime, let's encourage each other and work on what we can: positive body language, improved focus, and doing all the little things right."

Phoebe had said something similar during January camp: "Jo always has a plan. Our job is to control the things we can and accept the things we can't."

This sounded so much like the Alcoholics Anonymous serenity prayer—and so entirely unlike Phoebe—as to be borderline alarming. Emma was starting to think Phoebe and Ellie sounded less like team captains and more like evangelicals when it came to Jo Nichols. Or possibly robots. Ellie, at least, seemed to be offering sound advice: *Improve your attitude, focus on the little things, and stay positive.*

Emma closed her eyes, trying to blot out the worries threatening to hijack her brain in jet lag mode. The Algarve Cup was coming—a week of sunshine, sandy beaches, and competitive soccer. Emma would earn her starting spot back, enjoy some of the most beautiful beaches in the world with Jamie, and come home with another international tournament win.

No pressure, really.

She took a breath and called up the homework the national team's sports psychologist had given her when they'd met in January. Visualization was a powerful tool, as Mary Kate had reminded her. Emma pictured herself at the Algarve Cup, starting and playing in their first match against Norway; imagined herself running up the field in one of the movement patterns she'd practiced with Ellie and Jamie and the others; visualized herself slotting a through ball to Maddie, who slammed it past the Norwegian goalkeeper's outstretched fingertips into the back of the net. She could do this. After all, she'd survived the Great National Team Meltdown of '07. At least the current team liked each other and had each other's backs. Well, except Jessica North. But if one player had to be cut from the final World Cup roster—and she absolutely did—Emma's money was on her.

As Ellie had pointed out during one of her pep talks after the loss to France, they were Team USA. They would keep fighting as long as they had breath—which would be a really freaking long time, given how fit Lacey and Jo had made sure they all were.

#

For Emma, the team's headquarters for the Algarve Cup was a familiar temporary home away from home. The five-star resort sat on a bluff overlooking the Atlantic at the edge of the picturesque city of Lagos, Portugal, known for its miles of pristine beaches and stunning rock formations. The US team's first two games would take place 85 miles away in the small city of Vila Real de Santo António while the placement matches would be close to an hour away in Faro, but the extra driving was worth it. The resort had multiple hot tubs and pools—including one with a sandy floor—and its own football training facilities with two full practice fields that offered partial views of the ocean. It also had a golf course, game room, fitness facilities to rival most American gyms, and trails that led along the green cliff tops to a beautiful beach cove only a mile from the hotel.

On their first morning in-country, Emma and Jamie met for coffee and tea downstairs in one of the hotel restaurants, as had become their custom on national team trips. The best way to beat jet lag, they'd found, was to get up at a normal time right from the start. Travel mugs in hand, they headed out to the cliff-top trails, soaking in the morning sun and warmth, a sharp contrast not only from the coast of Brittany but also from the damp cold they'd left in Seattle a day and a half earlier.

"So how does it feel?" Emma asked as they walked, the careful space between them feeling particularly conspicuous after their alone time together in Seattle.

"Which part?" Jamie asked, smiling at her from behind aviator sunglasses. She was dressed in the blue Nike team sweats that matched her eyes and a white US Soccer snapback, and she looked so strong and gorgeous that Emma experienced a not-uncommon jolt of elation at the realization that this amazing woman was *her girlfriend*. "The jet lag part or the luxury hotel part?"

"Are you trying to say that my apartment isn't the height of luxury?" Emma huffed, swinging her hip into Jamie's. But gently—wouldn't do to make her splatter tea all over her team sweats, nor would Emma dream of spilling her own coffee even if they hadn't just flown halfway across the planet. Supposedly you acclimated to a new time zone an average of one hour per day, which meant she and Jamie should be used to Portugal's time by the third and final group match. Great. Just what you needed when you were fighting for a starting spot. The only good thing was that the other players were in the same boat—except for those who, like Taylor O'Brien, hailed from the East Coast, three full hours closer to Western Europe.

"Whatever. You know your apartment is amazing," Jamie said.

"Amazing enough that you might want to, I don't know, share it with me?" Emma asked, keeping her voice teasing. That way if this went sideways, she could pretend she had been joking. Because that was obviously the mature, adult way to handle asking your girlfriend to move in with you.

"What do you mean?"

Damned aviator sunglasses—Emma couldn't tell what Jamie was thinking from the tone of her voice alone. "In the off-season," she explained. "We don't get all that much time together, and I hate losing even a single day with you. Besides, you already spend most of your downtime in Seattle."

"I don't know," Jamie hedged, chewing her lip as they walked, the sun rising at their backs. "It hasn't quite been a year, Emma. Don't you think it's a little too soon?"

"I don't, but apparently you do," she said, trying to keep her voice light.

"Emma…"

"No, it's fine." She gestured with her coffee cup in a way that even she could see demonstrated an absolute lack of fineness. She softened her voice. "It's just hard to be apart, you know?"

Jamie nodded and reached for her free hand, squeezing it gently. She didn't let go, either, just held on as they walked, a fact that went a long way to making Emma feel less like an idiot for bringing up their living situation.

"Can we say that we'll spend as much time together as we can without calling it moving in together?" Jamie asked. "Because I've never actually lived on my own, and if I do get a contract from the federation next month—"

"You totally will," Emma assured her.

"—then I think I'd like to get an apartment in Portland, maybe one that's walking distance to the stadium. It's not that I don't want to keep moving forward with you, because I do. I've just never had my own space before."

"That makes sense," Emma said. And it did. She'd known all along that they were at different places in their lives and careers. Jamie was just starting her national team journey, whereas lately Emma had felt like hers might be winding down—whether or not she was prepared for it to do so. She tried to think of a subject change, settling eventually on an old favorite. "Anyway, are you ready to see your boys go down?"

Jamie glanced at her sideways, but Emma stared at the path ahead of them, willing her girlfriend silently to accept the face-saving pivot. Manchester United and Arsenal were due to meet in the sixth round of the FA Cup the following week on the same day the US was scheduled to play Iceland in their third and final group match. Emma wasn't sure yet how they would manage to see the game, but this wasn't something they could wait to watch on DVR back in Seattle. For one thing, someone was bound to tell them the score, seeing as they were currently in Europe, football capital of the world. For another, Emma had no intention of bypassing the opportunity to rub Arsenal's inevitable loss in Jamie's face.

"Dream on," Jamie said after a moment, elbowing her lightly. "As if ya boys even have a chance."

"Um, your boys are the ones who only won two out of their first eight matches, not mine."

"That was like five months ago. We're ahead of you in the tables, in case you hadn't noticed."

"By one point!"

"Yeah, well, you lost to Swansea City. Swansea City!" Jamie repeated, laughing.

And yes, United's performance the previous weekend had been unfortunate. "Whatever. One point, Maxwell."

They walked on, holding hands and sipping their caffeinated beverages, and Emma felt surprisingly content despite the fact Jamie had shot down her invitation to move in together. She'd been willing to wait before without even a friendship between them. A Jamie who loved her and wanted a future with her but still wanted a chance to succeed on her own? That, Emma could definitely wait for.

Playing time on the national team, on the other hand, not so much.

She didn't start against Norway, which was fine. Totally fine. The smile stretching across her face as she cheered for her teammates against a typically ultra-physical Norwegian side did not resemble a grimace in any way because she was TOTALLY FINE. When Norway took a

1-0 lead late in the first half on another error by newbie defender Lindsay Martens, it was all Emma could do not to glare at the coaching staff. Jo might like offensive prowess in her outside backs, but the decision to put Martens, a lifelong striker, in at left back against a quality opponent like Norway so soon after her abysmal performance against France risked damaging Martens's confidence irrevocably. Not only that, but this squad wouldn't rebound easily from a repeat of the previous year's disastrous finish at the Algarve.

The first half went from bad to worse when, in injury time, Steph went up for a header at midfield, crashed into a Norwegian player, and landed awkwardly. The ref blew the whistle for the foul, and the Norwegian immediately started to argue. Emma could see her point. There hadn't been that much contact. But Steph didn't get up as Emma expected her to do. Instead, she rolled onto her back and lay flat, her knees bent as she stared up at the sky. Maddie knelt beside her and leaned in close, one hand on Steph's. But only for a moment—whatever Steph said made her immediately rock back on her heels and gesture urgently toward the bench.

Crap. That did not look good.

Jo apparently agreed because as the team's trainers jogged onto the pitch, she barked, "Max! Warm up."

Jamie jumped up from her position at the other end of the bench and started warming up, her movements practiced and sure. If she was nervous, it didn't show. Probably she was just excited to play.

Emma knew that feeling. She missed that feeling.

Silence descended over the mostly empty stadium while the trainers examined Steph. After a short discussion, they helped her rise and hobble toward the bench, her gait uneven.

"It's her back," Emma heard the head trainer tell the coaches while her intern grabbed ice bags and a wrap from the kit.

Jo glanced down the sideline to where Jamie was warming up. "Maxwell! You're in."

Even as Emma worried over Steph—she'd been out for three months before the Olympics with a lumbar disc issue—she couldn't help being excited for her girlfriend. She watched, biting back an unprofessional smile as Jamie checked in with the fourth official and waited to be waved on. The center ref had barely lifted her hand when Jamie sprinted toward the center circle, kicking up her heels the way she always did when she subbed into a game. It was endearing, and Emma temporarily forgot her own frustration at riding the bench. Jamie was in the game, and Emma didn't think she was the only one who felt better about their chances.

The ref blew her whistle to end the half less than a minute later, and the two teams filed off the field and into the tunnel that led beneath the stands. The American players were quiet as they headed for the locker room they'd been assigned, their shared frustration at the game's physicality and the current score obvious in the set of their shoulders and the snap in their steps.

Steph was waiting in the locker room when they reached it, her face grave as she reclined on a training table, ice secured to her lower back by an Ace wrap. She tried to smile at her teammates, but understandably, it came out as more of a grimace.

"How are you doing?" Emma asked, pausing beside her.

"Peachy," Steph said.

"You'll do anything to get out of fitness training,

huh?" Maddie said, leaning in to muss Steph's hair.

"You know it." The veteran midfielder exchanged a weighted glance with Maddie, and Emma read what she didn't say aloud: Steph's back was wrecked. *Fuck*. Canada was only three months away.

"All right, athletes," Jo said from the front of the locker room. "Let's talk."

While the coaches leaned against the cheerful white and blue tiled walls, the players launched into a venting fest over the first 45 minutes of the game. Jo stood near the dry erase board still littered with colorful magnets from their pre-game talk. She projected her usual calm unflappability as the players hashed out the match's on-field dynamics, until finally, at a lull in the conversation, she jumped in.

"I've got to tell you, you put together a decent half, even if the score line doesn't reflect that fact," she told them. "The other coaches and I saw some good things out there, so keep doing what you're doing because it really is working. You just have to finish your chances."

The players murmured in assent, but no one sounded particularly energized. Everyone was probably remembering the previous year's utter collapse against Denmark in a similar stadium only an hour's drive away. Of course, they'd been down by *three* at halftime of that game. But the stakes were considerably higher now. If they couldn't beat Norway in front of 500 mildly interested spectators, how did they plan to win the World Cup in front of tens of thousands of fans who would consider anything less than first place a failure?

"Come on, guys," Ellie said, glancing around the room. "You heard Jo. Keep doing what you're doing out there. We just need to win the first fifteen minutes. If we can get an early goal, we're back in it and the momentum swings our way. Be patient. The opportunities will come."

Emma blinked at the national team captain, unaccustomed to seeing her midway through a game with neat hair and an unmarked uniform, her face free of sweat. Then again, Emma wasn't used to feeling so clean and untouched herself in the middle of an important match.

"Two things this team has never been short on," Melanie said, glancing around the room, "are effort and perseverance. Let's show them what we're made of, athletes. What do you say?"

This time the chorus of replies was stronger. They had come back in bigger games than this. In fact, the rest of the world had learned never to count America out. Look at the quarters in Germany four years earlier—down a goal and a player with no time left in extra time, and they'd still managed to pull off the win. And yes, that was years ago, and their more recent record wasn't doing their confidence any favors. But Emma knew that if they could wrench the lead back from Norway, then going down in the first half might turn out to be the best thing that could have happened. Resilience begat resilience, and struggle always made victory sweeter.

"All right," Jo said, motioning them in for a huddle. "We'll start the way we ended, except Martens and Perry, you'll take a rest in the second half. Blake, I want you in the middle and O'Brien on the outside. Ellie, I want you up top with Latham. Novak, you're in the ten. Any questions?"

For once with this team, there weren't. Emma exchanged a look with Jamie, who gave her a subtle thumbs-up. Emma nodded, adrenaline surging through her bloodstream. She was *back*, bitches.

Jo nodded around the huddle. "Go remind them who they're playing. Team, on three."

Ellie quickly counted it out: "One, two, three,

TEAM."

The chant echoed through the dressing room as Emma headed for the hallway, shaking out her arms and legs to keep them from trembling. Jamie was waiting in the corridor and fell into step beside her.

"Congrats," she murmured as she bumped Emma's hip, voice barely audible over the sound of their cleats thudding against the concrete floor.

"You, too," Emma said, watching her out of the corner of her eye.

"See you out there." And then Jamie was jogging ahead, briefly outlined by bright sunlight at the end of the dim tunnel.

Win the first fifteen, Emma thought a little while later as she waited for the whistle. She felt the usual pressure on her bladder as Ellie and Maddie lined up on the ball, but she knew it would pass as it always did. She smiled, feeling the warm Portuguese breeze teasing at the curls that somehow always managed to pull free of her ponytail. It was a perfect soccer day, and she was about to shut down the front line of Norway, one of the USA's oldest and most bitter rivals.

Bring it, she thought as the whistle sounded. *Fucking bring it.*

#

"Love-three," Ellie said, scowling, and held the ball to her paddle. Then she unleashed a serve that almost made it past Emma. She managed to tip it back over the net, but Ellie was ready and crushed the return.

"One-three," she said smugly, preparing to serve again.

Morning sunshine shone in the wide windows, lighting up the resort's game room. The coaching staff had given them the morning off after their come-from-behind win against Norway the previous day. Jo's substitutions had worked out beyond well. Ten minutes into the second half, Ellie had scored a header on a beautiful cross from none other than Taylor O'Brien. Seven minutes later, Jamie had driven into Norway's penalty area only to be tripped from behind. Ellie had slotted the resulting penalty kick into the right side netting to win the game for the US.

With the morning off, Emma could have slept in this morning. But she and Ellie were both early risers, so they'd met for coffee and "a friendly game" of ping pong before breakfast and sight-seeing with the rest of the team. One game had turned into two, and now they were rounding out the best of three. Why Emma hadn't predicted this spontaneous tournament was a mystery, really.

Despite her best efforts, Ellie went down early in the third and never managed to recover. Emma couldn't resist teasing her when the older woman slammed her paddle down at the end of the match: "I bet you went through a ton of tennis rackets."

"I probably would have," Ellie admitted, "but my parents refused to buy any more after I broke the first two."

"Is that how you became a one-sport woman?"

"Pretty much. You can't really break a soccer ball."

Coffee cups in hand, they left the hotel and headed toward the water, following the same path Emma and Jamie had taken after breakfast most mornings that week.

"It's funny that you get worked up over ping pong but not over being benched," Emma commented, subtly stretching her hip flexors as they walked.

"What makes you think I don't get worked up over riding the bench?" Ellie asked.

"I just mean you seem so calm. Like yesterday—you psyched everyone else up at halftime, and then you came off the bench to win the game."

"It was a team effort, Blake. You know that."

Emma sighed. "Jesus, Ellie, you're only proving my point. How do you stay so positive all the god-damned time?"

"I'm not positive *all* the time," Ellie said. "Ask Jodie. I call her and text her at all hours with my rants. I think for me, the key is to vent those emotions in a safe space without letting them spill over onto the team or, god forbid, the coaches."

Emma sipped her now-cold coffee, pondering Ellie's words. Jamie wasn't exactly a safe person to vent to because she was also fighting for a spot on the team. As a rostered player who had been a regular starter for years, Emma would feel awkward complaining about playing time to Jamie, who only had a handful of caps to her name and no guarantee there would be more in her future. Emma knew Jamie thought some of the veterans were entitled, and she didn't want Jamie to associate that quality with her.

"Jo says we all need to accept our roles," Ellie added, "and that's completely right. We win as a team and we lose as a team. But that doesn't mean I'm not going to fight to get the role I want. Besides, you know as well as I do that the lineup is in flux right now. This is the last real chance the coaches have to make any tweaks. By this time next month, they're going to have to decide who gets to go to Canada and who doesn't."

That was one of the primary reasons the US played in the Algarve Cup: to evaluate personnel. They came back to Portugal every year not for the palm trees and ocean vistas but for the opportunity to face top teams that knew how to play against them. In a little over a week of tournament time, the US gained experience with different styles of play, diverse lineups, and a variety of game day scenarios. There weren't many opportunities in the women's game to play in an international final, which was why the Algarve was so important to the team's development. This tournament was the closest they could get to a dress rehearsal for the World Cup.

But Emma didn't want to think about the World Cup right now, not when she wasn't sure game to game if she would be on the pitch.

"Who do you think Jo will start tomorrow against Switzerland?" she asked.

"With three games in six days, I bet she changes thing up," Ellie said. "I don't think Martens is going to see daylight anytime soon, though."

"Same," Emma agreed. She doubted Lindsay would receive another call-up until after the 2016 Olympics—if even then.

They walked on, discussing possible lineups for the remainder of the Portugal matches. Jo wasn't the kind of coach who played the same 11, game after game. Unlike Marty, who had preferred to let the starters figure things out on their own, Jo shifted the team's style depending on their opponent. That often meant switching up the personnel as well.

"I like that about her," Ellie said, "even if it means I'm not always on the field. Jo doesn't keep forcing a square peg into a round hole. She actually swaps it out for a round one."

"Wait. Am I the square peg in this scenario?" Emma demanded, faux outraged.

"No, you idiot. I am." Ellie winced slightly as the trail roughened underfoot, pausing to stretch her quads.

"Old much?" Emma teased.

"Another five years and you'll be where I am, and then we'll see who's laughing."

Five years—another full World Cup cycle plus one. Would Emma still be playing? Would Ellie? She would be thirty-eight, so it didn't seem likely. Tina Baker was the only player Emma had known to make it that long, and she seemed happy enough to have her soccer years behind her. Or maybe *happy* was the wrong word. More like too busy taking care of multiple tiny human beings to miss her former jet-setting soccer superstar lifestyle.

Anyway, five years was a long way away, Emma reminded herself a little while later as she and Ellie turned and headed back to the hotel. She would do well to focus on the here and now if she wanted yesterday's return to the starting lineup to be more than a blip on Jo and Melanie's radar.

CHAPTER FIVE

In Emma's opinion, their match against Switzerland was a much better showing for the team. Not only because she started and played the entire game but because—*finally*—the offense seemed to be finding its groove. Well, not in the first half, which remained scoreless. Switzerland's defense was well-organized for the first 45, but Emma could tell it was only a matter of time before the US attack found the seams and broke through. Sure enough, in the second half, Ellie came in to score two goals in ten minutes and assist Maddie on a third.

Ellie wasn't the only person to find her offensive groove. There was the minor business of Jamie and Emma each assisting on one of her goals. Jamie's assist was a perfectly lofted ball from outside the box that found Ellie's head in front of the goal, while Emma's contribution was less flashy but counted just as much. She'd intercepted a pass at midfield when all of a sudden, muscle memory took over. She passed to a checking Maddie, got the ball back, and dribbled into open space. When Ellie called for the ball, Emma sent her a neat through pass and watched, delighted, as Ellie one-timed it past the diving keeper.

Emma was on the board! She'd actually added offensive points to her stat sheet, just as Jo had asked of her.

"Nice job out there, Blake," Melanie said after the game, clapping her shoulder as Emma cooled down. "Looks like those extra practice sessions paid off."

They really had. Which she shouldn't be surprised by. To make it to this level, she'd had to eat, sleep, and drink soccer for years. It only made sense that she would need to continue to grow in order to stay at the top level of the game.

Game three against Iceland didn't go quite as well, and not just because Emma didn't start again. The US needed a win or tie in their final group match to advance to the finals, and in theory Iceland shouldn't present much of a challenge, given they were ranked 20th in the world and the US had never lost to them. But the island nation's players were strong and athletic, and their intention was clearly to challenge for every single touch. If an American player held the ball too long, Iceland didn't hesitate to put her on the ground. As a result of the constant pressure, the American players seemed a step off throughout the game.

With Steph out indefinitely with her reinjured back, Jamie got her second start in a row. Emma was happy for her—until partway through the first half when the other team's center back took Jamie down for the second time in ten minutes. Emma jumped up from the bench with the rest of her teammates—except Jessica North—to protest the foul, but she was probably the only one on the sideline who had to fight an urge to charge out onto the field and head-butt the Iceland center back Zinedine Zidane-style. Fortunately, Jamie wasn't injured. She allowed Angie, who had been given a rare start, to pick her up and dust her off, and the game resumed. Maddie did manage to "accidentally" elbow the whor—*the Iceland center back* in the face a few minutes later when they both went up for a cross, so at least there was that.

When Emma went in during the second half, she gave as many elbows as she received, though she was careful not to take any risks in the American defensive third. Iceland earned more yellow cards (three) than shots on goal (two), but they didn't score. Neither did the US, much to their own frustration. Still, they were through to the tournament's final, where they would play none other than France, who had gone 3-0 during group play. Even more impressively, they'd managed to defeat Japan—Olympic silver medalists and the reigning World Cup champions (*ugh*). No doubt about it. France was hot right now.

For the second time in six months, Emma realized, the American team would have the opportunity for nearly immediate revenge against a team that had defeated them. This time, unlike at the International Tournament of Nations in Brazil, the US would come out on top.

She hoped.

#

During the brief forty-eight hours between the final group match and the championship, a new team mantra emerged: "Score in the first 45." The only time all year they'd managed a goal in the first half had been against England the previous month, so this seemed like a good objective to rally around.

Jamie alternated that mantra with her own slightly longer recitation, intended for Emma's ears only: "Danny Welbeck scored the winner to knock United out of the FA Cup!"

For the first time in a very long time, Emma found she had zero urge to break team time rules with her annoying girlfriend.

"The first time in what, like, nine years?" Jamie teased as the team's charter bus carried them to Faro for the match against France. "Because that's how long it had been since Arsenal won a match at Old Trafford, baby!"

Emma didn't point out that Jamie was basically admitting that United was the better team, nor did she remind her seat mate that United had won 11 out of the 15 previous matches between the two sides. Instead, she clapped her noise-canceling headphones over her ears and pointedly stared out the coach windows at the wide ocean vista. While she might secretly have wished that United had never traded Danny Welbeck, she was happy to let Jamie brag about her Premier League team's victory if it would distract her from her nerves. Actually, Emma wasn't *happy* about the boasting. But she wasn't going to burst Jamie's Arsenal bubble, easy as it would be to do so. She was going to be a good girlfriend and listen to her psych-up mix—recent dance music and a few power ballads—while she visualized the upcoming match. Because like Jamie, she had received word at breakfast that she would be playing the full ninety today.

Her focus was, as usual before a big game, on defense. As her college coach used to say, "Offense wins games, but defense wins championships." Emma's primary responsibility (no matter what Jo thought) was to make sure France didn't score. Her secondary role was to start the build-up from the back. Back in the day, the American attack had centered on long balls launched up the field. Under Jo's leadership, however, the focus had shifted. The current coaching staff privileged technique and tactics over 50-50 balls, possession and patience over forcing the attack.

Emma's visualization exercises were aided by the fact they had faced France so recently. She could easily picture individual French strikers like Sophie Durand, the team's leading scorer. Could see herself beating Durand to a through ball, closing her down one-on-one, blocking her wicked shots. She made sure to visualize herself in the attack, too, contributing the way she'd practiced at January camp and beyond. Because if you didn't believe you could do something, you probably wouldn't be able to do it.

She managed to ignore Jamie and focus on her internal preparation right up until the bus pulled up to the stadium in Faro. She had played here a handful of times, most recently in a 2012 loss to Japan that came almost exactly halfway between losing to them in the 2011 World Cup final and beating them at the 2012 Olympics. Coming in third at the Algarve after losing to Japan that year had seemed like a near catastrophe until last year's actual catastrophic finish. Fortunately, the US was back on track again, back in the finals with momentum on their side—if you didn't count the minor hiccup of their tie with Iceland. Emma chose to focus on the big picture, the one where they had won 8 out of the last 12 Algarve Cup championship titles. Last year's performance and the loss to Japan were mere blips on an otherwise stellar record.

In the locker room, the players changed into cleats and stowed their gear, talking and laughing amongst themselves while the team's pre-game mix played on Bluetooth speakers. When everyone was ready to hit the pitch, Jo called them into their pre-game huddle. They stood in a loose circle, arms around each other's waists and shoulders, while Jo wrote a quote on the dry erase board: "Even if you're on the right track, if you sit still, you'll get run over." This was the same quote she'd shared at their very first team meeting after replacing Craig. She underlined it now and joined the circle between Melanie and Henry, the offensive coach, gazing at the players one after another.

"You've all heard me say before that in sport, as in life, there's no looking back. There's only moving forward. To that end, I challenge each of you to face this game today with a clean slate. Leave what happened in France where it belongs: in France." For a brief moment, Emma thought the coach's gaze might have lingered on Jamie, but she couldn't be sure. "You've done all the preparations and made all the adjustments we've asked you to. Now it's just a matter of putting it all together. Oh, and scoring in the first 45, of course. See you on the pitch, athletes." And she led the coaching staff from the room.

Ellie waited until the door closed to declare, her gaze as piercing as Jo's had been, "This is our chance to avenge more than last month. This is our chance to wipe away last year's pathetic showing, to move forward into the amazing future I know is waiting for us. Let's go out there and win the first fifteen minutes, and then the next fifteen, and then the next."

Across the huddle from her co-captain, Phoebe added, "We always do better when we score early, so let's get on the board right away, girls. You do that, and I'll give you a clean sheet, guaranteed."

Emma could feel Phoebe's confidence and Ellie's optimism flowing through the team, moving from one person to the next, filling them with the indefinable sensation she'd always associated with victory. They were going to win this match, she could feel it. France had no idea what was about to hit them.

They screamed out a cheer, and then they were filing out of the dark underbelly of the stadium and onto the freshly mown field, newly painted lines white and gleaming in the afternoon sunlight.

Before warm-ups, Emma performed her pre-game rituals: jogging to the goal on their assigned half, readjusting her shin guards, and plucking a few blades of grass from inside the six to test the wind. Today, the rituals felt more significant. She had always known her time in a US uniform was limited, but now she could feel the ephemeral nature of her chosen profession in her heart, in her stomach, in her bones. A week, a month, a year from now she could receive the news that she was no longer on the squad, and all she would be able to do was nod and say, "Thank you." For the chance to represent her country at the highest level; for the opportunity to be part of something so much larger than herself.

But not today, Satan. Today she had a game to win.

Warm-ups dragged. All Emma wanted to do was play, for fuck's sake. She could see France warming up on the opposite end of the field, their collective body language confident and relaxed, the looks they sent the US players smug and more than a little condescending. Emma gritted her teeth and tried to focus on her teammates as they lunged and stretched, as they played keep away, as they worked on passing patterns and small-sided games. She jumped in place during the requisite national anthems, humming through France's La Marseillaise because whether it was due to the previous month's loss or more about Jamie's teenage trauma, she was starting to really dislike all things French.

And then, finally, FINALLY, it was time for a last team cheer in front of their bench.

"Let's show these biatches where to shove it," Jenny Latham declared, and everyone laughed.

"Win the first forty-five," Ellie said, gazing around at them one by one.

She was back in the starting lineup too, and the confidence in her look and bearing was palpable.

"Get on the board early," Phoebe added, her game face fierce. "Team on three. One, two, three, TEAM!"

Emma jogged toward their defensive end with Lisa, Taylor, Ryan, and Phoebe. As usual, they gathered at the top of the penalty area and did their own cheer: "Hold the line!" While Phoebe continued on to the goal to execute her pre-game ritual pacing of the goal-mouth and spitting into her gloves, Emma took her place in the center beside Lisa. Jamie was on her way toward midfield, but paused to smile at Emma. She nodded back, face set. Once she was in game mode, she rarely smiled. Instead, she channeled her energy into being the fiercest, most badass woman she could be.

Jamie, she was pretty sure, understood.

The referee, a woman from Romania, lifted her whistle, and Emma felt it—that familiar sharp urge to pee. Then the whistle blew, and the game was on. As France dropped the ball back, Ellie led the pressure charge, forcing the French players to dump the ball all the way back to their keeper to start a slow build-up from their own box. The US kept the press on—so much so that Maddie got called for her first foul less than a minute into the game on a call that Emma thought was questionable at best. Both players had been going for the ball, and really, the contact had been incidental, hadn't it? Obviously, the ref didn't see it that way because she called Maddie over and gave her a verbal warning while both teams looked on in semi-amazement. Maddie was practically laughing, and she rolled her eyes at Emma as she turned away from the overly-officious referee.

They were professionals, though, Emma reminded herself as France prepared to restart, and as such were fully aware that there was no accounting for some refs. Better not to worry about what—and whom—you couldn't control.

France took advantage of the ridiculous call to launch an offensive off the free kick, but Emma cleared the in-swinger easily out to Taylor, who started the attack up the left wing. A moment later, France intercepted a long ball out of the midfield, and soon they were driving back down toward the US goal. A whistled handball on Jordan Van Brueggen gave France their second dangerous free kick in the first three minutes of the game, and Emma began to doubt her earlier certainty about the game's outcome. She lined up at the top of the eighteen as Phoebe shouted orders, relieved when Durand's notoriously dangerous free kick skipped harmlessly over the end line for a US goal kick.

While the center ref was undeniably whistle-happy, her bad calls went both ways. Just past the five-minute mark, France's right back used "too much" arm extension during a shoulder charge against Gabe—in the ref's opinion. Emma didn't actually see the need for a whistle, but no one asked her. Besides, she would take the bad call against France to even out the crappy reffing odds.

Jo called something from the sideline, and Jamie jogged over to take the free kick a few yards off the corner of the eighteen. While the referee inserted herself even more into the game by lecturing Jordan and her French counterpart for jockeying for position near the twelve, Lisa caught Emma's eye.

"Get in there," she said. "I've got the counterattack covered."

"Yeah?" Emma asked, already starting toward France's penalty area.

"Yeah," Lisa said. "Go get 'em, tiger."

Emma and Ellie exchanged a nod as they set up

between the six and the twelve. Then Emma looked back at Jamie, standing with her hands on her hips, waiting for the ref to cease her annoying posturing. Their eyes met and this time, Jamie didn't smile. Her nod was decisive. Emma knew before the referee blew her whistle exactly where the ball would be.

Sure enough, the high-pitched tweet had barely finished when Jamie took two graceful steps and launched the ball into the box. Emma sprinted past her defender to the near post, intercepting the ball on the six. Her vision narrowed, her hearing dimmed, and the only thing she focused on was connecting her forehead with the arcing ball and flicking it on toward the goal. All it took was a slight redirection, and the ball sailed past the wrong-footed keeper and into the back of the net.

Holy shit. Emma leapt into the air, swinging her fist upward as she shouted, "Fuck, yeah!" She had just scored her first ever goal for the national team! Why hadn't she done this sooner? It felt awesome!

The American fans erupted—or maybe that was the bench, given that the stadium was mostly empty—while the team converged on Emma, laughing and hugging her for varying amounts of time. Jamie hugged her for an extra-long moment, and Emma could practically read her mind. *Just like we practiced.*

"Gooooooooallllll!" Ellie and Jenny said in unison, smacking her back so hard Emma thought she might lose her breath.

Taylor O'Brien hung back from the celebration, but as they jogged back to their defensive end for kick-off, Emma pulled her into a side-hug. Now that this particular newbie wasn't stealing her playing time, Emma could admit it: Taylor deserved her starting spot. She was a beast at both ends, and in the past year, Jo and her NWSL coach had managed to mold her into a more measured, controlled monster. Emma was psyched she was on their team, especially as the first half wore on and Taylor continued to occasionally run over a French player.

France was playing slower than the last time they'd met, Emma noticed. Was it because the field was grass instead of turf? Either way, the US was possessing the ball better this time around. Still, France didn't pull back just because they were down a goal. They continued to press and take advantage of US errors with quick runs down the flanks and probing balls through the seams of the defense. Except there weren't many seams to exploit. Phoebe, Lisa, and Emma had been playing together in the center of the back field for years, and they ran a tight ship. The defense stayed organized, and then, just before halftime, Jenny Latham received a pass from Maddie in the center of the field, accelerated past four French players, and, from the top of the box, coolly slotted the ball into the right corner of the goal. It was her first goal since an ankle injury in Brazil, and Emma was thrilled to see her back on form. She honestly didn't think they could win the World Cup without Jenny healthy and in a good mental space.

At half time, the mood in the locker room was more than upbeat. It was practically effervescent.

"Excellent work out there," Jo said once they'd settled down. "That second goal illustrates exactly what we're after: building up from the back, passing to feet, and, you know, a little bit of individual brilliance."

The team laughed and applauded Jenny, who rose and bowed with a flourish.

Jo shook her head, smiling. "Credit where credit is due. Congratulations to Emma, as well—that was her first goal for the program. Way to go, Blake!"

As her friends and teammates chanted her name and

slapped her back, Emma couldn't have stopped the smile that split her face if she tried. She didn't try. No wonder strikers loved scoring so much. It was totally addictive.

Jo spent the next few minutes on the dry erase board, sketching squandered US opportunities and using magnets to illustrate holes in the French defensive organization. At last she capped her pen and regarded them. "I want you to keep the pressure on in the second half and really work to spread the field even more." She pointed at the quote on the board. "Whatever you do, don't stop moving forward. Keep pressing their backs and looking for seams."

The second half, unlike the first, turned out to be a defensive battle. That, and a battle to see who could avoid drawing a red card. Emma typically ignored the officiating, but this referee was making that impossible. She seemed nervous, as if she were auditioning for the World Cup, too. Maybe she was performing for a FIFA inspector in the stands. Otherwise, Emma had no idea why she would stop the match repeatedly to lecture players on nonexistent infractions, or track the ball so closely that she managed to get hit more than once. Actually, maybe both teams were simply aiming for her. Certainly no one seemed particularly concerned when she took a shot to the face a few minutes into the second half.

A little while later, Taylor shoulder-charged a French player, Desjardin, in the box. Desjardin immediately flopped in the way that all European players seemed to know instinctively how to do. It seemed possible that they really did take acting classes, as the old joke suggested.

Emma tensed as Desjardin rolled dramatically and the referee blew her whistle. Fortunately, she only signaled a goal kick before turning away. *Whew*. That could have been ugly.

While Phoebe set up the goal kick, Emma gave Taylor

a high five and said, "I love your aggressiveness, O'Brien, but tone it down when you're in the box, okay? Especially with this ref."

"Right," Taylor said, nodding quickly. "Got it."

She didn't get it, though, judging from what happened in the 80th minute. They were still up by two and getting close to wrapping up the match when Taylor slide-tackled Desjardin just inside the penalty area. Once again the French player embellished the contact. But whether it was a makeup call or simply another bad call in a very long list, the referee blew her whistle and pointed to the center spot.

A penalty kick. *Fuck.*

Taylor was resting on her knees, hands on her thighs as she stared up at the ref in disbelief. Emma resisted the urge to browbeat her—*I told you to cool it in the freaking box!*—and, instead, lifted her up by her jersey and walked her to the top of the box.

"Don't worry," she said, squeezing Taylor's shoulder. "That wasn't a penalty kick. This ref is showing off for someone, that's all."

"But you told me to go easy in the box and I didn't," Taylor said, her eyes flashing genuine remorse as Sophie Durand placed the ball on the spot and took two measured steps back.

"No looking back, remember?" Emma said, setting one foot in front of the other at the edge of the eighteen. "Only moving forward. Let it go and focus on the rebound."

"The rebound?" Taylor echoed.

The whistle blew, and before Emma could respond, Durand stepped forward and ripped a low, hard shot to the left corner—only to see her shot blocked by a fully extended Phoebe Banks. Apparently the bank was closed today, Emma thought gleefully as she raced toward the rebound and cleared it out over the distant sideline.

"Thanks, Blake," Phoebe said, slapping Emma's outstretched hand.

"Right back at ya, Phoebes."

"Oh my god, I'm so sorry!" Taylor said as a French midfielder jogged out to take the throw-in.

"It's fine." Phoebe's tone was surprisingly kind. "You made me look good, kid. Now mark up on number nineteen!"

France continued to press for the next ten minutes, but Phoebe easily shut down the handful of opportunities they earned. Probably the ref's only widely approved whistle on the day was when she blew the final three tweets of the match. Emma jumped a little in place and then quickly moved to shake hands with the French players in her immediate vicinity. She was about to turn for the bench when she felt a hand on her shoulder, the only warning she had before Jamie swept her into her arms and twirled her around, laughing.

"We did it!" she said, grinning at Emma.

She was so excited, and all at once Emma remembered: This was Jamie's first international tournament with the senior national team. "We did it," she agreed, smiling up at her girlfriend. "Way to go, James."

Jamie smiled back at her, happy and—*wait*, was she actually thinking of kissing Emma? Because it almost looked like…

At that moment, Maddie joined the hug uninvited, squeezing them both against her sides. "Boo-yah, ladies!"

"Clam jammer," Emma murmured into her best friend's ear.

"Someone's gotta keep you two professional," Maddie whispered back.

As they headed to the bench, Taylor caught up with Emma. "Thanks for talking me down earlier," she said, the same awkward uncertainty from before back now in spades.

"No worries," Emma said, elbowing her. "That's what teammates are for. But remember not to make contact in the box. Most foreign players will embellish it. It must be part of their training."

"Got it," Taylor said.

This time, Emma hoped she actually did.

The post-game huddle was happy but low-key. They'd played way too many games in way too short a time, and honestly, Emma suspected that the strongest feeling most of them were experiencing was relief. If they had lost to France twice in a month this close to Canada, the sports media would have pounced with headlines ranging from benign—"US falls again to France" —to critical: "US woes continue in World Cup year." With this victory, they'd earned themselves a temporary reprieve from the apocalyptic-leaning critiques of the international sports press.

It wasn't easy to be the number one—er, *number two* team in the world, but Emma could take the hot seat if it meant she got another chance at World Cup gold. She was pretty sure the rest of the team could, too. They'd better, because after today, there were only eighty-nine days to go until Winnipeg.

EIGHTY-NINE DAYS.

Tick, tock, mothafuckas, indeed.

CHAPTER SIX

Jamie opened her eyes and blinked up at the unfamiliar ceiling. Where was she? Stifling a yawn, she focused on the sound of Britt snoring nearby in a single bed practically touching hers in what might well be the smallest hotel room she had ever seen.

Oh, right. Paris.

Where she was on any given morning had become a recurring exercise in disorientation over the past few months. First LA, then France, England, Seattle, Portugal, England again, and France. *Again.* At least she was adding tons of new stamps to her passport. After the match this afternoon—Champions League quarterfinals—most of their Arsenal teammates would board a train bound for the Chunnel while Jamie and Britt caught a flight back to LA for the national team's final residency camp before the World Cup. Camp would already be in full swing when they arrived. They would only be a day late, but still, it was almost enough to make Jamie wish she hadn't agreed to compete with Arsenal in Champions League. A contract was a contract, though, and when she'd made the decision, she hadn't known she would end up starting for the national team.

Starting for the national team. Like, for real? That shit was mindboggling.

The Algarve Cup felt a little like a dream now. After her own injury struggles, Jamie would never wish harm on anyone, especially not one of her idols from when she was younger. But as Melanie had said to her in Portugal, injuries often paved the way for other players to step up and show the coaching staff what they had to offer.

"You're on the right track, Max," Mel had told her at training the day after they'd tied Iceland. Despite the outcome, Jamie felt like she'd played well. She'd nearly assisted on two goals—first to Maddie on a shot the midfielder had struck over the crossbar, and later to Jenny, whose shot had ricocheted off the left post. In the game against Switzerland, she'd notched a picture-perfect assist to Ellie's prolific head. That was enough to keep her going through a hundred near misses.

"You think so?" she'd asked Mel.

"I know so," her favorite assistant coach had replied. "You're starting in the final."

A thrill had shivered its way across Jamie's spine. "I am?"

"You are." Mel had held up her hand. "Play well tomorrow and the six is yours to lose, kiddo."

Jamie had slapped her hand possibly a bit too hard, judging from the coach's wince, but she couldn't help it. A national team coach had just told her that she was on her way to a starting position on the freaking World Cup team! Jamie had never been one to play things cool. She wasn't about to start now.

To be honest, she'd never seen herself as a defensive midfielder. She would definitely be following in vaunted footsteps. The defensive midfield role had been made famous by such greats as Arsenal's French star, Patrick Vieira; Chelsea standout and, again, Frenchman Claude Makelele; United's Irish talisman Roy Keane; and American legend Michelle Akers—who, not incidentally, had graduated from Emma's high school in the '80s. Not bad company to find oneself in.

Smiling a little now, she stared up at the ceiling of the tiny hotel room, remembering how it had felt to hoist her first-ever trophy with the national team, knowing that she had contributed substantially to the win. Amazing, that was how it had felt. It still did a week and a half later, too.

She had Emma, a starting spot on the national team, money in the bank, healthy family members—what else was there, really? Except maybe a loss today so they wouldn't have to face Lyon in the semis. Arsenal had somehow played PSG to a scoreless tie in North London five days earlier, which meant a win or a tie (with at least one away goal) today would put them through to the Champions League semis.

Jamie didn't *really* want to lose to Paris, of course. Besides, it wasn't as if she could avoid Lyon forever. FIFA had just announced that France had been selected to host the 2019 World Cup. Every single game would be on grass—which would be a massive improvement over Canada—but the opening match and the finals would be played in Lyon, of all places. Jamie would probably be better off trying to exorcise her demons before the next World Cup cycle.

Beside her, Britt started awake with a snort. Slowly, she stretched her arms over her head and twisted until both of her shoulders popped.

"Gross," Jamie said, snickering. Keepers and their shoulders usually operated on a love-hate basis, and Britt was no exception.

Her friend blinked at her sleepily. "You're awake?"

"Yep." Jamie refrained from commenting on the near impossibility of sleeping through her roommate's nasal reverberations. No need to make Britt feel bad for something she couldn't help.

"Did I tell you Allie set up an appointment for me at a sleep clinic in DC?" Britt asked as she sat up in bed and scrubbed her hands through her bed head. "She's worried I might have sleep apnea and won't wake up one morning."

"Is that even a possibility?" Jamie asked, kicking her covers off and sliding her feet over the edge of the bed.

"Allie thinks it is. Apparently a friend of her family died from it in his 40s."

"Crap," Jamie said, stepping into her slippers. That wouldn't be Britt, would it?

"At least I wouldn't have to worry about that for a while. Do you want the first shower? Assuming you can manage to spend less than an hour in there."

"Ha, ha." Jamie threw one of her pillows at Britt, but the other woman snagged it out of the air and added it to her existing pile.

"I'm serious, James. Team breakfast waits for no one."

"Twenty minutes, I promise."

Britt reached for her phone. "Whatever you say."

Their 40s seemed like eons away, Jamie thought a few minutes later as she soaped up in the hotel room's narrow shower stall. For a moment, she let herself daydream about what her life would look like in a decade and a half. Would she and Emma be married with kids and a mortgage and all the other trappings of the American Dream? More importantly, would their trophy case contain matching

World Cup gold medals? Or maybe not *more* importantly. Probably she shouldn't mention that little mental slip to Emma, her potential future wife and baby mama.

First things first. For now she had to focus on playing soccer with a team she hadn't seen much of since the fall. Fortunately, everyone else was in the same boat. Arsenal's preseason had just started, and since Jamie hadn't gone home between the Algarve Cup and Champions League, she had gotten in a few days of practice with her former side. She was currently missing preseason with the Thorns, but she would be lucky to play in even a quarter of her NWSL club's matches this season. Jo had already informed the players that once the final training camp began at the beginning of May, they were US Soccer property first and foremost. Those who made the final cut, anyway.

Aargh. She couldn't wait until the roster announcement next month. And yet, at the same time, she really, genuinely could.

She shut off the water and reached for her towel. Maybe breakfast with the team would keep her over-active worry center occupied.

Britt pretended to frown when Jamie emerged from the bathroom. "That was only fifteen minutes. Did the hotel run out of hot water?"

"Fuck off," Jamie said, but she was smiling as she reached for her team sweats. It was game day, and they were about to have breakfast in the City of Lights. Not bad, really. Not bad at all.

#

They won. They actually beat PSG at home in Paris. The game had been tied until the 75th minute when Arsenal earned a free kick in PSG's defensive third. At the whistle, Jamie lofted the ball into the box, aiming for

Jeannie's prominent head. A simple flick from Arsenal's tallest player, and they were up. PSG pressed like crazy for the next 15 minutes, but Arsenal managed to preserve the shut-out. Britt was brilliant, a point their coach made sure to stress during the team's brief field-side celebration.

"Way to go, bud," Jamie told her best friend a little while later as they caught a cab to the airport. "You were totally amazing! Two shut-outs in a row against one of the best clubs in Europe—yeah, boy!"

Britt ducked her head, and Jamie felt sure she was about to downplay her role in their victory. But then she lifted her chin and grinned. "I was pretty amazing, wasn't I? I believe—"

"—that we have won!" Jamie finished with her, laughing. They repeated the phrase, and then, as the cab delivered them to Charles de Gaulle and they checked in, they repeated a variation on a common theme: *I believe we have arrived! I believe we are checked in! I believe this terminal is interminable! I believe our flight's delayed!*

Actually, that last one wasn't funny. Because while Jamie was psyched they'd beaten PSG to advance out of Champions League quarters, she was less impressed by the fact that their late arrival at camp would now be even later, judging from the flashing sign at their gate. It didn't even offer a new estimate, only the wildly unhelpful word: DELAYED.

While Britt plopped into a chair at their gate and called Allie, Jamie paced the carpeted strip near the window, waiting for Emma to pick up. But she didn't, so Jamie contented herself with a message: "Our flight is delayed. No new ETA. I'll keep you posted. Love you!"

She'd already texted Emma about their win practically before the game was even over, and Emma had sent back tons of happy emojis. This message would garner significantly fewer of those, Jamie would bet.

A call to the national team manager yielded better results. Within half an hour, their tickets had been changed and they were on a new flight that would get them into LA—sooner, actually, thanks to a shorter layover in Vancouver, BC.

"What about our luggage?" Jamie asked Fitzy, thinking of her Algarve Cup medal—her first with the senior side. She knew she shouldn't have checked it.

"It'll arrive eventually," Fitzy said. "And when it does, we'll have it delivered to the training center."

"Okay," Jamie said, trying to tamp down her worry. It was only a hunk of medal, after all, and she already had a sizable collection of similar hardware taking up space in her childhood bedroom.

She and Britt shouldered their carry-on bags and sprinted across the airport, only pausing long enough to check the gate assignment Fitzy had given them. They reached the new gate with only a few minutes to spare, and after checking in with the desk agent, they were jogging down the empty gangway and stepping onto the nearly-full flight. Their seats weren't together on this flight, so they waved and went to find their separate rows on the huge jet. Jamie had barely buckled her seatbelt when the plane pulled away from the terminal and began its long, slow trek to the runway.

"On a new flight, one stop in Vancouver," she texted to Emma, glancing at her hastily printed boarding pass for the new flight number to include along with the new arrival time. "See you sooner! Love you."

Emma's reply came quickly: "Love you too! Safe flights!" And she typed a string of emojis, including hearts, an airplane, and more than one pair of crossed fingers.

A flight attendant gave Jamie the kind of pursed-lips look that only a French woman could pull off, so she turned her phone to airplane mode and slid it into the seatback pocket in front of her. No need to piss off the flight personnel at the outset of a transatlantic flight. Emma knew her whereabouts, and that was what mattered. As it turned out, Emma wasn't only afraid to fly herself. She was also afraid for anyone she loved to get on an airplane.

"Not exactly convenient, given our jobs involve a teeny, tiny bit of travel," Jamie had murmured into Emma's ear the morning Emma confessed this fact. It had been their last full day off before the Algarve, and they'd been lying in bed in Emma's apartment, snuggling before a scheduled workout with her trainer. Jamie's arms had been around Emma's waist from behind while Emma had nestled back against her, the little spoon to Jamie's big spoon.

"Ugh, I know," Emma had said, sighing. "I'm sorry, but I can't exactly help that my uncle got himself killed on an ill-advised ski trip."

"Okay, but what are the odds someone else in your family would die in a plane crash?" Jamie had asked.

Emma had literally slapped her hands. "Don't say that! Jesus, talk about a sports jinx."

Athletes were seriously the most superstitious people in the world.

Despite Emma's next level fear of flying, Jamie didn't worry too much about crashing. The odds of being in a car accident were significantly higher, which was one of the reasons she hadn't let her parents drive down to see her at her first residency camp in LA a year and a half earlier. That, and she hadn't wanted to be distracted. But flying, to her mind, was one of the perks of being on the national team. You got to wake up in one part of the world and go to sleep in another. Plus the view of the earth from above couldn't be beat. She loved looking down on the world below and imagining the people on the ground who might be gazing up at the jet's contrails. Flying was awesome. Except when there was turbulence. Then she disliked it just as much as the next person, assuming the next person wasn't Emma.

This particular flight was smooth, and soon Jamie's eyelids were drooping, the past couple of months of travel catching up to her as she'd suspected they would. Good thing she'd remembered her travel pillow. A kink in her neck wouldn't do, not when she was about to commence the last round of try-outs for Canada. In the next few weeks, the coaches would make their final selection. Out of the twenty-five athletes invited to Carson this time, two would have their hearts broken.

Two out of twenty-five—those were actually higher odds than Jamie would have liked.

Still: "Congratulations! The six is now officially yours to lose," Melanie had told her after they'd beaten France two weeks earlier.

Jamie replayed the statement now, remembering Mel's proud smile as she'd clapped Jamie on the back. Remembering, too, her and Emma's private celebration once they got home from Portugal. Not only had Emma regained her starting role (at least temporarily), but Jamie had somehow managed in the space of a single year to ascend from the cut list to a coveted position on the top squad in the world.

Flying was the least of their worries, really.

#

After spending the last couple of months mostly in Northern Europe, it was nice to be warm again, Jamie thought as she and Emma strolled along the boardwalk at Hermosa Beach. The coaches had given them the morning off ahead of an afternoon scrimmage against the under-17 boys' national team, and when Emma had invited her out to breakfast, Jamie had jumped at the chance to be alone with her. They'd eaten at a restaurant so close to the beach they could hear the rhythmic hum of the surf, and Jamie had savored the chance to be themselves away from team rules and the constant teasing of their friends. Being a couple on the national team really wasn't for the faint of heart.

The sun was still rising over the buildings that bordered the beach, and only a few people were out jogging or riding their bikes along the boardwalk on a Wednesday morning in late March. With their identities masked by baseball caps and sunglasses, Jamie felt safe reaching for Emma's hand as they walked along the sand-dusted pavement.

Emma, however, glanced at her quickly and pulled her hand away. "What are you doing?"

Jamie swallowed a sigh. "Sorry. I just thought…"

Emma maintained a careful bubble of space between them as they walked on. "You know we can't risk it."

"We held hands in Portugal," Jamie pointed out. "And France, and England, and—"

"That was different."

"How?"

"It just was, Jamie. Drop it, okay?"

Emma had been doing that lately—making unilateral decisions about their public presentation and then getting irritated with Jamie when she dared disagree. While Jamie could appreciate that Emma was gobs more recognizable than she was, it still stung to be rejected.

"You know," she said, choosing passive aggression because that was a language that Emma spoke fluently, "this is the beach where I threw away the bracelet you gave me."

Jamie's trashing of the bracelet wasn't news. She'd admitted her rash action shortly after she and Emma had started dating, apologizing profusely even as Emma had assured her the action was well-deserved. But now Emma looked at her, eyes unexpectedly vulnerable.

"It is?" she asked, her voice slightly stricken.

And, great, another regret to add to Hermosa Beach. Maybe Jamie would be better off steering clear of this area in the future. "Yeah. Sorry," she said for the second time in as many minutes.

"It's fine." Emma looked away, fixing her gaze on the ocean where seagulls swooped and a handful of surfers in full wet suits chased the early springtime waves.

Jamie wished she were out there in the wide, steady ocean instead of walking on the boardwalk with her silent girlfriend. Emma was probably just tired. Jamie was, that was for sure. Crisscrossing the globe was bad enough, but residency camp had been even worse, starting out as it had with the final fitness testing of the year. The last beep test until 2016 was something to celebrate, but first you had to get through it. Jamie had done okay, but her legs were still tired from playing PSG and then traveling halfway around the world all in the same 24-hour period. She could have done better. But then again, she could have done worse, too.

The six is officially yours to lose. Melanie's words had become something of a mantra to Jamie, motivating her through the two full days of fitness testing and the two-a-day training sessions that had followed. This was their first morning off all week, and she'd been looking forward to spending quality time with her girlfriend. Why then did it feel like Emma was intent on pushing her away?

"Is there something we need to talk about?" she asked, and then immediately regretted the question. This beach did not have good history when it came to her relationship with Emma.

"No," Emma said, but she didn't sound convinced.

What the hell? Maybe Emma had changed her mind. Maybe she'd decided that Jamie was too much of a distraction and had nearly cost her a starting role on the national team. Maybe she was trying to find the right way to let her down easily—

Jamie's phone rang, interrupting her panicky spiral. She pulled it from the back pocket of her skinny jeans and checked the screen. Why was the national team manager calling her on their morning off?

"Hello," she said cautiously, looking away from Emma's curious gaze.

"Hi, Jamie," Fitzy said. "Do you have a minute?"

"Sure." Jamie tried to sound upbeat. Fitzy could call her without there being anything wrong, couldn't she? The last time she'd called had been to let Jamie know the airline had found her missing luggage from Paris. Apparently it had traveled to Asia and back before finally arriving in LA. Good thing the National Training Center had extra equipment for athletes in exactly her position—and good thing, too, that she had packed her cleats in her carry-on. That was a habit she'd developed during her youth national team days, back before she was on the senior side with access to the "boot room" and as many pairs of her favorite cleats as she could ever wish for.

"I received a call a little while ago from a Michael Hollis at Nike," Fitzy continued. "He was asking for your agent's name and number."

Nike? Holy shit. *Holy effing shit!* But—"I don't have an agent."

"I am aware of that fact. And now so is Mr. Hollis. Would you like me to email you his contact information?"

"Sure. Thanks," Jamie said, pacing away from Emma.

"Done. But a word of advice, Ms. Maxwell: Find an agent before you return Mr. Hollis's call."

"Okay," she said, nodding quickly even though Fitzy couldn't see her. "I will. Thanks!"

She ended the call and waited until her email alert went off before turning off the display. Then she pocketed her phone and all but skipped a few paces down the boardwalk. Nike! Wanted to talk to her!

"What was that about?" Emma asked, her tone neutral as Jamie caught up to her.

Too excited to hold a grudge about their earlier disagreement, Jamie relayed the national team manager's message. "Can you believe it? Nike actually called for me!"

"Of course I can believe it." Emma seemed willing to let bygones be bygones, too, judging by the next words out of her mouth: "Do you want me to call Joel and see if he would be interested in repping you?"

Joel Rubin was Emma's agent—and Ellie's and Maddie's, too. Jamie had met him briefly the year before when he'd "popped by" her contract negotiations with the Thorns as a personal favor to Ellie.

"Are you serious?" Jamie asked. "Do you think he would actually be interested?"

"Doesn't hurt to try. If his client roster is full, he should be able to point you to someone else at his agency."

That was a nice way of saying that Jamie might not be

high enough profile for Joel, but that a more junior agent at Sparks Sports Management could probably be convinced to take her on. Given that Rubin's firm was legendary in professional sports circles, even a junior agent would be a sign that Jamie had officially arrived.

As Jamie hesitated, Emma added, "You don't get what you don't ask for."

Or, as the soccer saying went, 'You miss a hundred percent of the shots you don't take.'"

"Okay, then," Jamie said. "That would be cool. Thanks, Emma."

"You're welcome." She checked her own phone. "We should probably start heading back soon, especially if you want to check out the pier."

To be honest, Jamie didn't particularly want to go back to team time. Not yet, not when they hadn't been alone like this for what felt like forever. But as she paused, a hand slipped into hers.

"What are you doing?" she asked quickly, glancing up at Emma.

"I'm holding my girlfriend's hand," Emma said, her chin tilted at a stubborn angle that Jamie recognized more from the soccer field than from their personal interactions. "If that's okay with you?"

"You don't have to if you're not comfortable, Emma. I won't be offended."

"Are you sure about that?"

Well, no, she wasn't. But she didn't want to be offended, so. "Yes," she said, bracing herself for Emma to release her hand.

Instead, Emma leaned in closer, her shoulder brushing Jamie's, and said, "You really are too good to me, you know that?"

She smiled, breathing in Emma's familiar scent: cucumber shampoo mixed with dark roast coffee. "Somebody has to look after you. Might as well be me."

Emma laughed, the sound rumbling against Jamie's shoulder as she tugged her along the boardwalk back the way they'd come. "Too bad you didn't feel that way about the bracelet I gave you."

"Dude! I totally regret that now."

"To be fair, you couldn't have known then that we'd end up together."

"I don't know. I might have guessed."

Emma stared at her as they passed a surf shop with a rainbow sign. "I thought you didn't ever want to see me again."

"I didn't at first," she admitted. "I was so angry with you. But that passed. Eventually, I realized that more than anything else, I missed you."

Emma was quiet. Then she said, "I missed you too. I thought I would see you in North Carolina at the College Cup finals your junior year, but you weren't there."

"Wait." Jamie frowned, doing the math in her head. "Why were you there? You graduated the year before, didn't you?"

Emma shrugged. "No, actually, I had to take a leave of absence for the Olympics. I came back to UNC that fall to finish up."

Jamie remembered that College Cup. For the second year in a row, Stanford had qualified as a number one regional seed, this time with an 18-1-1 record. Unlike the previous year, they'd made it out of the round of 16, defeating Portland in the quarters to earn an invitation to the College Cup in North Carolina. But Jamie and Britt hadn't gotten a chance to participate in Stanford's attempt at a championship run. The day before the first round of the NCAA tournament, they were on an airplane headed for Chile, where they would compete for—and eventually win—the 2008 U-20 Women's World Cup.

"Britt and I were bummed not to be there," she said, "but obviously there was no choice."

Emma nodded. "You can't turn down a national team call-up, no matter what's going on in your regular life."

"You missed your last high school match, didn't you?" Jamie remembered.

"I did. I used to think the federation was hazing us on purpose, testing us to see how we would respond to being pulled between club and country. Probably it was good training, but in '08 it meant I missed seeing you."

"Did you even want to see me then?" Jamie asked.

Emma side-eyed her. "Of course I did. I always want to see you, Jamie."

She said it so easily, so certainly, that Jamie felt the last vestige of her hurt from earlier melt away. "I always want to see you too."

"Duh," Emma said, nudging her with her hip.

Jamie laughed. "Jerk."

"You know you love me."

"I do," she agreed, and tightened her grip on Emma's hand as they walked on, seagulls cawing while the ocean surf gleamed in the morning sun.

CHAPTER SEVEN

"I'll take the meeting," Joel said. "But you owe me, Emma."

Emma grinned into her cell phone and offered Jamie, who was pacing nearby, a thumbs-up. "In a few months, Joel, you're going to be thanking me for this opportunity."

Her agent laughed. "Ellie just told me the same thing."

"She did? When?"

"I was hanging up with her when your call came through."

"So you were already planning to meet with Jamie?"

"Can't put one past you," Joel deadpanned. "I see why you're the captain of the nerd squad."

"Whatever. Thanks anyway," she said, rolling her eyes. She'd been working with Joel for close to eight years now, since just after she'd made the permanent roster. He could be kind of a dick at times but mostly in a good way.

"You're welcome, Emma. Talk to you soon."

That was certainly true, Emma thought as she ended the call. Media scrutiny and fan pressure would mount in the coming weeks, and Joel's USWNT-related work obligations would rise commensurately. If the US did manage to win the whole thing, his phone would ring off the hook for months afterward.

"So? What did he say?" Jamie asked, dropping onto the bench beside her.

They'd stopped at the Hermosa Beach Pier to people watch despite the fact that the number of surfers, fisher people, and tourists out and about on a weekday morning was not high. Jamie had been too distracted by Fitzy's call to focus, though, so Emma had decided to check in with her agent. With the scrimmage scheduled for the afternoon, they might not get another chance soon.

"He said forget it. No way." She slipped her phone back into her fleece pocket.

"Emma!"

"Of course he'll meet you." She gave Jamie the same thumbs-up she'd offered her less than a minute earlier.

"Yes, but what did he *say*?"

"That Ellie had already called him to recommend you. Which seems curious, seeing as I've been with you all morning, and I could have sworn you hadn't talked to her."

"I might have texted her while you were in the bathroom," Jamie admitted, looking adorably sheepish as she hunched her shoulders into her hoodie and blew noisily into her to-go cup of tea. They'd stopped for more coffee and tea along the way, though they'd both gone with decaf this time.

"Strike while the irons are hot?" Emma asked.

"No, I was just excited. I mean, it's Nike, Emma! Like, holy crap!"

Emma smiled into her coffee cup. Sometimes she

forgot how new all of this was for Jamie. In Emma's mind, Jamie's place on the national team was a done deal because of course she should have a roster spot. She was like a quarterback, a talented Drew Brees type who saw the entire field. With one look, she could predict the next play and the play after that. But in point of fact, Jamie's current contract was still only temporary, which was why she'd never needed an agent before.

"By the way, thanks," Jamie added, her voice softening. "I appreciate everything you and Ellie are trying to do for me."

"You deserve all the things, Jamie." She shifted closer on the bench, sipping her coffee. Decaf wasn't the same as regular, but it would have to do. She didn't want to be too hyped up when they played the U-17 boys.

"You deserve all the things, too," Jamie said, smiling into her eyes with a look that clearly and unabashedly communicated her feelings.

"Well," Emma drawled, invoking her Great Aunt Olga's Minnesota accent, "we do."

"Dork," Jamie said, laughing.

"Nerd." She sipped her coffee and rose reluctantly. "Come on. Time to make the donuts."

Jamie sighed and followed her toward the street. "If only donuts were on the approved diet!"

One day they would be able to eat whatever they wanted, but Emma doubted they would appreciate their newfound freedom. They would only miss the days when they had to sneak away in order to enjoy a rare breakfast alone together.

Humans, she thought as they walked back to the team van they'd signed out that morning. Apparently the grass really was always greener.

#

In hindsight, Emma should have known not to push it. Holding hands on a nearly empty sidewalk was one thing, but snuggling together on a popular pier for all the world to see? That hadn't been wise, as became evident when her notifications went off just before they left for the scrimmage. Jamie glanced at her, but Emma only tilted her screen away and silenced her notifications. Not before she'd seen the alert, though: a new #Blakewell post on Tumblr from a college student, her self-proclaimed biggest fan. Someone had apparently noticed them on the pier because there was a photo of them exchanging a sideways smile, bodies pressed too close together to be considered strictly friendly.

She racked her memory on the way to the practice fields, trying to figure out who might have taken the photo. She hadn't noticed anyone tailing them at the beach this morning. Whoever it was, he or she must have been sneaky. That, or Emma had been too caught up in Jamie's giddiness over the Nike call to notice much of anything else. Still, just because the teens on Tumblr had seen the photo didn't mean the Twittersphere had taken note, she reminded herself as she tucked her phone into her kit bag and dropped it by their designated bench. Fingers crossed her other "biggest fan" wouldn't notice.

During warm-up, she sized up the teenage boys running through drills on the opposite end of the field. Except for a couple of smaller players, the entire team stood head and shoulders above the women's side—except Ellie and Phoebe. And even the team captains were shorter than at least a handful of their youthful opponents. The boys were bigger, which basically guaranteed that the women would struggle against them not because male players were better or smarter but because they were faster and stronger. Even at this age, the boys physically outmatched adult female players in almost every way.

Why had Jo even scheduled this scrimmage? Ellie had expressed support, as had a few other players, but Emma was worried about morale. If the press got wind of the story—"Top-Ranked Women's Team Falls to Boys' Team" (because Emma could almost guarantee the outcome)—the usual narrative would be spun, and then Reddit and 4chan and every other shitty male site on the Internet would add their own misogynistic spin. It wasn't even the misogyny Emma minded. It was the glee of the fat, out-of-shape, unathletic men who laughed at stories of women losing to boys, as if the score somehow reflected women being put in their place when really all it did was highlight the biological reality of men's superior strength and speed—even when said men were skinny teenagers who didn't even need to shave yet.

To say that Emma wasn't feeling positively predisposed toward the male of the species that afternoon was an understatement she could acknowledge. The faceless, nameless minions on the Internet who harassed her at every turn and threatened to do more than simply harass women like Jamie—those men she could do little about. But one pimply little son-of-a-bitch who dared to take a potshot at her girlfriend on the fields where Emma had been playing while he was still in diapers? Oh, she could definitely do something about him.

Although if she had it to do over again, Emma could admit, she probably would have handled the situation differently. But when the teenaged dickweed slide-tackled Jamie at midfield, pushed off her, and turned away, a smug smirk on his lips, Emma didn't think. She didn't have time to fully process the fact that Jamie was on the ground clutching her leg, or that the boys' youth national team coach serving as referee was blowing his whistle long and shrilly before something compelled her forward. She definitely wasn't thinking as she covered the small space between her and the boy, except to debate how to punish—no, *hurt*—him.

In the end, her brain couldn't choose between slide-tackling him from behind (even though play was dead and he didn't have the ball) and punching him in the head, so her body did the easiest thing it could come up with during her moment of indecision: She shoved him from behind, both hands flat against his back as he walked away from Jamie's prone figure.

He didn't fall, but he definitely came close. As he whirled around, shock and something else (was that fear?) contorting his face, she heard herself snarl, "I'm going to kick your ass, you little fucker! Come on!"

He barely hesitated before surging toward her, clearly about to take her up on the fairly explicit challenge to his masculinity in front of dozens of their teammates. Instead of backing down like her rational mind was quietly suggesting might be the better option, Emma moved forward to meet him.

Fortunately, calmer minds prevailed. Not hers or the boy's, but one of his teammates held him back while Ellie stepped between them and Maddie grabbed Emma from behind.

"Stop it!" Maddie hissed. "Chill out, Em!"

As she struggled against Maddie's grasp, one part of Emma's brain noted that Maddie was sounding more and more like Angie every day. The rest of her conscious mind was busy trying to manage the fury still coursing through her.

"Blake! Sideline! *Now!*"

The commanding voice cut through the fog of rage clouding Emma's sight. She finally understood that cliché—it really was as if a thin layer of red overlay everything in her field of vision. At least, until she realized that the person shouting at her from the sideline was none other than Jo Nichols, the coach with the power to leave her off the World Cup squad.

Jesus, what was wrong with her? The little bastard who had taken Jamie down wasn't a child, but he wasn't an adult, either. She stilled immediately and glanced at Maddie. "I'm okay. I'm good. You can let go."

"You swear?" Maddie asked, eyes narrowed.

She nodded. "I swear. I'm good, Mads."

Maddie released a breath and eased her grip. "Okay, then."

Emma glared one last time at the boy—too bad looks couldn't kill, really—and turned to stalk toward the sideline, anger punctuating every step. As she passed Jamie, she made the mistake of looking at her girlfriend, who by now was back on her feet. Emma started to ask if she was all right, but the look in Jamie's eyes stopped her. *Doh.* Jamie was pissed—at her, apparently. Perfect.

"Sit," Jo said as she reached the sideline, pointing to the opposite end of the bench.

Emma bit back the words threatening to spill out—*But he deserved it! Did you see what he did to her?*—and headed for the end of the bench. Now was not the time to speak, not when she couldn't control what might come out.

"Damn, Rocky," Angie commented as Emma passed. "Didn't know you had it in you, bruh."

"Yeah, well, remember that the next time you think about pissing me off," she snapped.

Angie's eyes widened, but she didn't reply. No one else on the bench said a word, either, as Emma claimed her spot and slouched down, hands hanging between her knees. *Fucking little shit.* What the hell had that boy been playing at? Except Emma knew exactly why he'd fouled Jamie. She'd noticed him before the scrimmage watching the women warm up, elbowing his buddies and making comments that had a couple of the other boys snickering right along with him. An older boy, the team captain possibly, had told the trio off, but they'd only shrugged, not looking the least bit contrite. Some teenage boys didn't do well with being made to compete against female players, even if the women's team was ranked number one (okay, *two*) in the world. Maybe especially if they were one of the top teams on the planet. Jamie, a relative newcomer and one of the few women in the national pool with short hair and an androgynous build, made an easy target. Throughout the first forty minutes of the game, Emma had watched the boy jostle Jamie roughly, elbow her, and chop at her ankles before finally pulling out the dangerous—and illegal—tackle.

Emma knew, too, that her anger was outsized, that her reaction didn't completely match the offense. But she couldn't help it. The threat constantly hanging over Jamie as an out lesbian in the public eye was exacerbated by their relationship. Worse, it always had been. Emma had never forgotten how Justin, her ex-boyfriend, had shoved Jamie against a concrete pillar hard enough to bruise her ribs. Emma had tried to intervene but she was slighter then, built more for speed than power. Now, though, she could bench press her high school self's weight, and the kick-boxing classes she attended with Dani had taught her to be comfortable with the kind of physical contact that most girls and women were culturally programmed to shrink from. In fact, muscle memory from months of kick-boxing had probably taken over back there. He was lucky she hadn't laid him out with a well-placed roundhouse kick.

Then again, she was lucky, too, because there probably wouldn't be any coming back from that in the eyes of the federation.

Melanie knelt before Emma, blocking her view of the field, and touched her on the shoulder. "Walk with me, Blake."

Emma rose and followed the assistant coach down the sideline until she stopped well out of earshot of the rest of the team.

"You okay?" Melanie asked, her eyes more sympathetic than Emma would have expected.

She shrugged and glared toward the opposite bench, where the boy she'd shoved was currently being lectured by one of his coaches, too. "Not really."

"Do you want to talk about it?"

"These are people's careers, you know?" Emma burst out. She took a breath and folded her arms over her chest as she glanced back at the assistant. "This isn't some game."

"Well, technically, it *is* a game..." As Emma's scowl deepened, Melanie held up a hand. "Sorry, too soon. But you know, I saw it too."

Emma blinked. "You did?"

"Pretty hard to miss. And while I don't exactly condone your methods, I do think it was important that someone out there stand up for Jamie. Someone other than Ellie, preferably. Only, next time, remember that there are ways to take someone out that won't get you ejected."

"You mean...?"

"I mean the way you handled Beaumont at the

Olympics."

Emma's brow rose. Was a national team coach really counseling her to take on-field revenge in a way that wouldn't get her—or the team—in trouble? Then again, these were extenuating circumstances, and Melanie, as the players had gossiped about ad nauseum, had lived with another woman for most of the decade she'd been a USSF coach. She was a private person and didn't talk much about her home life, but at the same time, she wasn't exactly in the closet.

"I'll remember," Emma said. "But to be honest, I hope there isn't a next time."

"You and me both, Blake. You good now? Really?"

Emma nodded, feeling immeasurably lighter. Knowing that someone else had her back—and Jamie's—made a huge difference. "I'm good. Sorry I lost my shit out there."

As they returned to the bench, Melanie raised her voice. "Apology accepted. I don't want to see you lose it like that again, understood?" But she turned her head and winked where no one but Emma could see it.

"Absolutely, Coach," Emma bluffed back.

Melanie held her eye significantly before heading to the other end of the bench, where she conferred with Jo and Henry. The other two nodded and stared at Emma, who bowed her head in pretend contrition. If ever there was a next time, she would follow Melanie's advice and find a way to hurt the bastard legally, just as she'd done with the Canadian player who had stepped on Emily Shorter's head. Sixteen or seventeen was plenty old enough not to be a homophobic asshole.

When they shook hands at the end of the scrimmage—which the boys' team won easily, god damn them—Emma held her hand away from the one who had taken Jamie down and muttered, "*Fuck off*," loud enough that he couldn't miss it. She smiled thinly at the next player in line, whose Adam's apple bobbed nervously as she slapped his hand. Okay, so maybe some of them really were still just kids.

She tried to catch Jamie's gaze as the team met and cooled down, but her girlfriend avoided her. This wasn't surprising, given that she hadn't looked at Emma even once since the shoving incident. Still, shouldn't Jamie be glad that someone, as Melanie had pointed out, had stood up for her?

The silent treatment continued in the van. Jamie already had her headphones looped about her neck when Emma slid into the driver's seat, and refused to look up from her phone where she appeared to be scrolling through her music database.

Emma was tempted to make a grab for the phone, but as her earlier foray into reckless action hadn't gone particularly well, she opted instead to clear her throat. "Hey."

Jamie lowered her phone. "What?"

"Can we talk?"

"Apparently."

Emma decided to ignore her sarcasm. "I feel like I should say I'm sorry, only I'm not entirely sure what I'm apologizing for."

Jamie scoffed. "Are you serious, Emma?"

She felt herself bristling and tried to tamp down on the urge to defend herself in front of their teammates, who despite their own headphones and conversations she felt sure must be listening in. But the words popped out anyway, delivered in the acerbic tone that used to make Sam gaze at her in obvious disappointment: "In case you missed it, Jamie, I'm the one who stood up for you against that juvenile delinquent."

"I didn't miss it." Jamie looked down at her phone, rubbing at a smudge mark on the now dark screen.

"Then why won't you look at me?"

She expelled a short breath. "I didn't ask you to defend me, Emma."

"We're teammates. It's what we do."

That got Jamie to look at her. "So you're saying you would have gone all Mike Tyson for pretty much anyone out there?"

"I didn't actually hit him, you know."

"You had your fists up and you threatened to kick his ass!"

So she had heard that part. Emma hadn't been sure. "Saying and doing are two very different things."

"Are you going to answer the question?"

Emma blinked and looked away. "No," she admitted softly.

"No, you're not going to answer the question, or…?"

"No, I wouldn't have done that for just anyone." She returned her gaze to Jamie's. "The thing is, I wouldn't have had to."

"Excuse me? What's that supposed to mean?" Jamie asked, her voice tight.

"He went after you for a reason. You know that, right?"

Jamie shook her head. "On second thought, I don't think I want to have this conversation." And just like that she pulled the noise-canceling headphones over her ears and hit play on her phone.

Emma watched her for a second, toying with the tip of her ponytail. *God.* Why was this so hard? And why did they have to do this in front of other people? Too bad she couldn't drive the van away until all the stragglers had been accounted for.

Gently, trying not to alarm Jamie, she tugged on her headphones. "Hey."

Glaring at her, Jamie pulled them down again. "What?"

"I'm sorry, okay? I didn't mean to piss you off. But he can't just do that. No one should be able to get away with that. It's not fair."

Jamie took a deep breath and closed her eyes. As she exhaled, Emma thought she heard her murmur something. Then she opened her eyes and shifted in her seat toward Emma. When she spoke, her voice was so quiet that Emma had to lean forward to hear her.

"You didn't piss me off. It's just, what if his teammate hadn't held him back? What if Ellie hadn't been there? You could have gotten hurt, or thrown off the team, or both, and it would have been because of me."

"Nah, I could have taken him," Emma said. "What does he weigh, like a buck thirty soaking wet?"

Jamie shook her head, frowning. "This isn't funny, Emma. He was my problem to handle, and I would have except you didn't give me the chance."

"I was trying to help!" Why couldn't she see that?

"No," Jamie said, "you were trying to protect me. I don't need your protection, Emma. I'm fully capable of taking care of myself. Kind of been doing it for a while now."

But, Emma's mind insisted, *what if you can't?* She

swallowed the words and tried to focus on what Jamie was saying. At some level, she knew that Jamie's reaction had less to do with the kid on the other team and more to do with the assault in France, even if she wasn't sure exactly how the two incidents intersected. But she didn't have to understand the intersection to respect what Jamie was asking of her.

"Fine," she said after a minute, her tone grudging. "I won't throw down on your behalf ever again."

It took Jamie a moment to respond, as if she hadn't expected Emma to capitulate so quickly. "Okay, then. Promise?"

"I promise." Emma paused, thought of her stalker situation, and amended, "In theory."

"What does that mean?"

"It means I reserve the right to revise my statement in the future as required." God forbid the situation ever arose outside the soccer pitch… She pushed the thought away. Nope. Not going there.

Jamie shook her head. "You're infuriating."

"So I've been told."

As the last player finally settled into her seat behind them, Emma started the engine. This time she didn't intervene when Jamie lifted her headphones. She only kept her eyes on the road as she guided the van back to the hotel, trying to focus on anything other than aggressive, entitled men and punk-ass teenage boys.

#

Their talk in the van wasn't the only difficult conversation Emma had to face. At dinner, Jo stopped by her table. "Blake, a word in my room later?"

Emma swallowed her spoonful of vanilla yogurt. "Sure

thing."

"Text me when you're ready."

Emma nodded and watched the national team coach walk away. That couldn't be good, could it? Jo hadn't seemed angry, though, simply serious. So there was that.

Across the table, Jamie went back to jostling with Angie for elbow room, but her eyes still managed to ask Emma a clear question: *You okay?* It was the first time she had made more than cursory eye contact with Emma since the scrimmage, so Emma supposed she had Jo to thank for that. She shrugged subtly and Jamie returned the gesture.

Emma, at least, couldn't predict Jo's reaction to what had happened. Or rather, what Emma had done. Her parents had taught her and Ty to take responsibility for their actions, so that was what she would do. But the truth was, she wouldn't take back what she'd done even if she could. Sticking up for Jamie wasn't something she thought needed an apology. And while she understood that other people believed violence was never the answer—of course, they were entitled to their opinion—she didn't agree. Sometimes violence was absolutely the right answer, especially in a situation like today where Jamie hadn't done anything to trigger the stupid boy's aggression other than be herself. A self, incidentally, that took constant courage in the face of a culture that didn't value her identity.

And yet, most coaches weren't like Melanie because most coaches had zero tolerance for fighting. True, Marty had taken Emma's side when she'd taken out Beaumont. But that situation had been significantly different from this one, starting with the fact that Emma's retaliatory tackle had been perfectly legal and had happened during the run of play. Also, Beaumont was a fellow female professional whose dirty play had been opportunistic but not necessarily personal. The kid today, on the other hand, had taken a shot at Jamie because she played for a different team euphemistically, not literally.

She stalled for as long as she could after dinner, taking an extra-long shower and bingeing a couple of episodes of *Modern Family* with Maddie before finally texting Jo: "Is this a good time?"

"Sure," Jo replied. "Give me fifteen and come on up."

Emma bit her lip. Wasn't her kid staying with her? Hadn't she said something about her husband having a business trip or some such thing? Well, that was fine. Emma liked Brandon. At ten, he was still sweet and looked up to the women on the team, instead of acting all egotistical and smug like some of the boys from today.

Huh. Her antipathy toward men certainly appeared to be holding strong.

Jo's door was open a crack when Emma arrived, the metal latch wedged into the gap, so she only knocked lightly before pushing it open. Jo was sitting on the couch in the living area of her suite, laptop open before her. She looked at Emma over the top of her glasses and nodded toward a nearby chair.

"Have a seat," she said, tone neutral. "Just let me finish this email."

"Okay."

Emma sat down on the padded chair and tucked her feet under her, glancing around the room. Through an open doorway she could see Brandon asleep on a king-sized bed, and she wondered what it had been like for him to be uprooted suddenly from Virginia, the only home he'd ever known, and transplanted to Southern California. She didn't envy him that, nor did she envy him the prospect of being the only child of the USWNT's head coach. The American women had dominated the game for so long that they were expected to win every game they played and place high in every tournament they entered. The coach who failed to achieve gold in the course of a four-year cycle was panned by fans, the federation, and sports journalists alike. If they didn't win in Canada this summer, Jo could use the excuse that she had been brought on without enough time to make a real impact. But if they also failed to capture the gold in Rio the following year? Her job wouldn't be secure—assuming that it ever was.

"Okay," Jo said, setting aside the laptop. "Let's talk, Blake."

Emma waited, but the coach didn't say anything else, merely watched her with sharp eyes that Emma had often thought didn't miss much. She tried to wait Jo out, but finally the silence was too much. "What do you want to talk about?" she asked, relying on an open question—her go-to in situations where she didn't feel in control.

"How are things?" Jo asked. "I believe you met with Caroline at January camp. Was she able to assist you with some of your online issues?"

The subject matter threw Emma briefly—wasn't she here so that Jo could upbraid her for her conduct at the scrimmage?—but she tried not to show it. "Sort of. I mean, she offered some advice that was helpful. Basically, I'm no longer running my professional social media, and I've changed my personal accounts as well."

"But…?" When Emma frowned slightly, Jo added, "I thought I heard a 'but' in there somewhere."

"But there's really nothing anyone can do," Emma admitted.

"There isn't, is there?" Jo leaned forward, elbows on her knees. "We didn't have anything like that when I was playing. We had the press reporting on our major tournaments, of course, but until the '96 Olympics, we were barely on anyone's radar. The team didn't start having the kinds of problems you're describing until after '99, and even then, there was no social media to create the echo chamber we currently see."

"Sounds nice, actually," Emma said, half-smiling.

"It was." Jo paused. "I have a question. What went through your mind this afternoon when you went after that boy?" Despite the topic, she didn't sound critical. Rather, she seemed genuinely curious.

Emma cleared her throat and glanced at the sleeping child in the next room.

Jo followed her gaze and waved a hand. "Don't worry about Brandon. He could sleep through an earthquake. Oh, wait, I shouldn't tempt fate. Earthquakes are an actual possibility here, aren't they? I'm still getting used to the California thing."

"A little different from Virginia?"

Jo nodded. "Probably as different as North Carolina is from Seattle. But back to my question. What were you thinking about that made you react that way?"

She shrugged. "Honestly, I wasn't thinking. I literally saw red, and the next thing I knew I was shoving him. It was like my body took over, and I was just in there watching."

"Lizard brain," Jo said. "That's the term Mary Kate uses to describe the emotional state when fight or flight takes over. It definitely fulfilled an important evolutionary role when our species was less established, but it's not quite as useful these days."

Emma glanced down at her hands in her lap. Against her better judgment she said, "I'm sorry I lost control."

"I'm not. I mean, I am in the abstract sense," Jo clarified as Emma's gaze flew back to her. "Not because that kid didn't have it coming because while I will deny this if you ever quote me, let's face it: He more than had it coming. But mostly I'm sorry because I think I know what was behind your manifestation of lizard brain, and there's nothing I can do as your coach—or even as a friend—to make that part okay."

Unexpectedly, Emma felt tears threatening. As long as she was angry, she didn't have to feel what lay beneath the heat: a deep, abiding grief that Jamie, like so many other girls and women, was forever changed by what had happened to her. Grief that Sam had feared for her safety because of her relationship with Emma. Grief—and, yes, rage—that it might be happening all over again and there was nothing Emma could do to stop it.

She swallowed against the sudden tightness in her throat and looked down at her hands again, toying with the hem of her sweatshirt. "It's awful," she admitted, "knowing what happened to her and not being able to make sure nothing like it ever happens again."

"You're right," Jo said, nodding. "What happened when she was younger was terrible. But Jamie doesn't let it define her. She's worked hard to move on with her life and achieve her dreams, just as you have." She paused. "Have you talked with her yet about the online situation?"

"No, I didn't want to throw her off her game right now."

"I understand your reasoning, but I think she might be more resilient than you're giving her credit for, Emma. Besides, secrets aren't good for anyone."

"I know that," Emma said, a little irritated. She didn't tell Jo how she should handle her marriage or her child, did she?

Jo steepled her fingers. "Did you know that research shows that keeping secrets can impact not just your emotional well-being but also your physical health? The problem is that people don't just think about something they're keeping from others when they actively have to hide their secret. They also think about whatever they're hiding even when it isn't in danger of being found out. That's what adds the extra physical and emotional stress."

That… actually made sense. Emma thought of her father. The damage to his heart hadn't appeared overnight. It had taken months, possibly even years of stress to damage the muscle. Months and years during which he had spent more time away from his family than with them, months and possibly even years during which he'd had a secret affair that very nearly ended his marriage and had irrevocably harmed his relationship with his daughter.

If he had lived, she'd often thought, she would have eventually found a way to forgive him. If he had still been alive right now, she would have viewed him through a more empathetic lens than the self-righteous, black and white viewpoint she'd possessed as a teenager. She might not ever fully understand how he could have done what he'd done, but she wouldn't have held him to such high standards. The world was far more complex than she'd realized in high school.

"I didn't know that," she told Jo. "But I can't say I'm surprised."

"And yet…?"

"And yet, I still don't think this is the right time to tell her. I will tell her, and soon. But not before… just, not right now."

Jo eyed her a moment longer and then, finally, nodded. "Timing. I get it."

Emma was pretty sure she did.

"In the meantime, I'm going to ask something else of you," Jo said. "I want you to talk to Mary Kate about all of this. I don't mean Jamie's history or your current relationship, but about the harassment you've been experiencing. I've watched you play for a while now, Emma, and I've never seen you lose control like you did today. Bottling up your feelings is doing no one any favors, especially not asshole boys on the under-seventeen team."

Emma coughed out a laugh before slapping a hand over her mouth.

Jo looked at her over her reading glasses. "Again, if you quote me on that, I will deny it. Is that clear?"

"Perfectly," Emma said. "I actually met with MK in January, but I'll see if I can get another appointment before New Zealand." She realized what she'd said and flinched slightly. "I mean, before the end of camp."

"It's okay, Blake," Jo said, smiling. "You will indeed be on the roster for New Zealand. You've risen to the challenges I've thrown you, just as I believed you would. Despite your Rocky impression this afternoon, your spot on this team isn't in any danger."

Emma stared at her, the lump in her throat returning. "Thanks, Coach. Seriously."

"It's nothing you haven't earned. Good luck with balancing everything. I hope you know you can reach out for help at any time. That's what the team behind the team is for."

"I know." She rose. "I should probably be heading to bed."

"Sounds good. Don't be a stranger, Emma."

"I'll try not to be."

Their eyes held a second longer, and Emma wasn't surprised anymore to see the kindness and genuine caring alongside the strength and determination that had always defined Jo, both as a player and a coach. In addition to her work with the federation, she had managed the University of Virginia program for more than a decade before assuming her current mantle. Those who had played for her still sang her praises. She obviously cared about her players, possibly even as much as she cared about the game itself.

How lucky they were that the team was finally in the right hands, Emma reflected as she returned to her room. Then she caught herself. Now who sounded like an evangelical robot? It was possible she was starting to see the light where their head coach was concerned. Having her spot guaranteed didn't hurt, obviously. Now if only Jo would hurry up and make Jamie an official member of the roster. Once she did, Emma could come clean and there would be no more secrets between them.

Gulp.

As she stepped out of the stairwell, she pulled out her phone and typed Jamie a quick message: "Jo was great. Very understanding. Called it an attack of lizard brain and says my spot is safe." She added a gecko emoji, followed by, "Just wanted to let you know."

Jamie's reply came back almost immediately, just as Emma reached her room: "Glad to hear it. Also unsurprised because pretty sure your spot was never in question."

Emma paused in the hotel corridor. "I really am sorry about earlier."

This time, the reply took a bit longer. "I know. It's okay. We're good."

The size of the wave of relief that washed over Emma was a little embarrassing, really. "Good. See you in the morning?"

"See you in the morning," she confirmed.

"Sweet dreams, Jamie."

"Sweet dreams to you too, Em. Love you."

"I love you too," Emma wrote back.

Her throat tightened and she swallowed hard, remembering what Jo had said about Jamie's resilience. But what about Emma's resilience? She understood that what had happened to Jamie wasn't about her, but it wasn't entirely *not* about her, either. What had Jamie said on the phone one night when they were in high school? That France hadn't only happened to her. The damage was like concentric rings on the surface of a lake, extending out well beyond the initial point of contact to anyone and everyone who loved her.

In a matter of weeks, Jamie would be returning to Lyon for the first time since that initial point of contact. Emma was tempted to fly to France with her, but she had her commitment to the Reign to think about. She couldn't just take off for personal reasons, no matter how compelling those reasons might be.

As she closed the door behind her, Emma nodded at Jordan VanBrueggen where she lay in the bed by the window, reading her Kindle. The Lyon trip was still weeks away. For now, Emma should focus on getting through the rest of camp and the game against New Zealand. One day at a time was not only a helpful adage for alcoholics and other addicts. It was also a pretty useful slogan for athletes.

Sheesh. She was definitely drinking the Kool-Aid now. But that was probably a good thing, Emma thought as she turned off her phone and got ready for bed. After all, they had a world title to win. A cheer from her high school team popped into her head: *A team united can never be divided.*

One could hope, anyway.

CHAPTER EIGHT

"No way am I getting in there," Angie said, backing away from the tram door.

"Oh, come on." Maddie grabbed her hand and tugged her forward. "It's your size, Ange!"

Jamie exchanged a look with Emma, who shrugged in what Jamie read as resignation.

"After you," Emma said, waving toward the absurdly small elevator car.

"Let's do it," Jamie said, and ducked to enter the car.

The doors were only four feet high, according to Emma's guide book, and the seats inside each tiny elevator car—or "tram" as it was officially called—were also on the small side. They hadn't been settled long when the door slammed shut automatically and the tram began to climb. Jamie held her breath, expecting the swoop and whoosh of the Empire State Building or Seattle's Columbia Tower, but it never came. Then she remembered that the guide book had said the cars only moved at 3.7 mph. *Doh*—that was just cruel. Way to prolong someone's fear of heights.

And by someone, of course, she meant Emma.

"You okay?" she asked her girlfriend softly, rubbing a thumb over her wrist.

"Yep," Emma said, lips tight as she gazed at the concrete walls and metal spikes slipping past the tram's lone window.

Jamie had expected to see St. Louis as they climbed—seriously, why else would there be a window in an elevator?—but the view before them was decidedly interior. Only after they'd arrived at the top (indicated by a sign that read, "You've reached the top!"), abandoned their tiny elevator, and maneuvered up a narrow stairway did they finally reach a series of small, rectangular windows that offered a proscribed view of the world below.

After one look at the distant ground, Emma seemed content to share facts from the book while the rest of their group gazed out on the mighty Mississippi River, the city of St. Louis, and the surrounding countryside.

"The Gateway Arch is the world's tallest arch and the tallest man-made monument in the Western Hemisphere," Emma read, her eyes fixed on the book. "It stands 630 feet tall—"

"Wait," Maddie said, glancing between the view and Emma. "How can this be the tallest building? The Sears Tower in Chicago is twice as tall."

"Not the tallest *building*," Emma corrected her. "The tallest monument."

At that moment, the Arch seemed to sway, and Angie grabbed Maddie's hand. Emma looked slightly green too, so Jamie edged closer, hoping to provide reassurance without setting off her girlfriend's sensitive PDA alarm.

"It says here," Emma added, her voice surprisingly steady, "that the Arch was designed to sway up to eighteen inches in either direction in order to withstand earthquakes and winds in excess of a hundred and fifty miles per hour."

Angie ran a hand over her carefully coiffed hair. "Good to know."

Maddie flashed a smile at Emma. "Always pays to bring the nerd squad along."

"You know it," Emma said.

Jamie was impressed with how unafraid she appeared, especially since she knew that Emma disliked heights as much as Angie did. The Arch had not been high on Emma's list of local attractions (*ahem*), but she'd agreed to go when the coaches gave them the afternoon off. Getting out of her comfort zone was something Jamie knew Emma took seriously, and this trip offered that opportunity for both of them.

Playing for Arsenal had taken Jamie to every major city in the UK and a number of European cities as well, but there were still plenty of locales across the United States where she had yet to set foot. Places, in fact, she had never intended to visit. The increasingly bitter partisan divide between "red" and "blue" America meant that she had little interest in visiting states that had long sought to ban relationships like hers and Emma's or communities that actively legislated against people like her. Why would she want to contribute to local economies that refused to recognize her humanity?

It wasn't just the money aspect that kept her out of red states, either. She was a genderqueer lesbian who was sometimes mistaken for a man, and that could be a damning combination—particularly in conservative communities. The political divide in the so-called Union meant there were areas of the US she wasn't sure she would feel safe, looking like she did and loving whom she loved: Texas, Alabama, Oklahoma, and (ironically for a woman-loving-woman) both states that started with

"Miss." Dirty looks weren't violent in and of themselves, but there was no way to know whose hostility stayed on the surface and whose ran significantly deeper. A nasty look might just be a nasty look, or it could be the precursor to a violent act. That was why Jamie preferred not to travel to certain parts of the country. Why risk antagonizing the wrong person simply by being who she was?

And yet for all of her preconceptions, St. Louis, it turned out, was a Genuine Soccer City. This had become evident the night they arrived when they were greeted by the largest airport crowd Jamie had ever encountered. The hordes of preteen and teenage girls waiting at baggage claim with painted faces and handwritten signs had been a surprising but welcome sight. Most of the signs were for Lisa Wall, the "hometown" favorite who had played every minute so far of 2015 and would likely play many more minutes in the coming months. Lisa had moved to Southern California as a teenager to improve her soccer opportunities, but her extended family still lived in and around St. Louis, and Missouri still claimed her as one of their own.

Jamie and the other former U-23ers had smiled fondly as Lisa glanced around baggage claim, waving at familiar faces and pointing out local soccer club banners, her face alight with happy surprise. And then Lisa froze, her smile growing impossibly wide. She dropped her carry-on and sprinted across the tile floor, barely slowing before slamming into her boyfriend, Andre. His arms closed around her and he spun her around, both of them laughing as the crowd murmured its approval.

"Did you know he was coming?" Angie had asked.

"No," Jamie had admitted. "I had no idea."

She'd watched their reunion with Emma standing nearby but not too close, and she'd wondered: Did Lisa know how lucky she was that her relationship was officially sanctioned by the federation? It wasn't just a non-teammate relationship that US Soccer supported. It was two happy, shiny heterosexuals whose successful long-term relationship the federation could point to. Not to mention the person of color box US Soccer could check every time they included Lisa in a promotion or feature, as the defender had pointed out more than once.

But that sense of tokenism never survived meeting a little girl who looked like her, Lisa had confided. There had been a few players of color on the '99 team, but no starters in field positions that young girls of color could identify with. Serving as a role model for girls and other women who routinely received the message that they weren't enough—not smart enough, pretty enough, or good enough—because of their skin color kept Lisa from turning down promotional opportunities, she'd said, even when she felt like she was being used. The opportunity to do good was too powerful to ignore.

Jamie and a few other lesser-known players had hung out in the background while Lisa greeted the crowd, posing for selfies and signing jerseys, posters, T-shirts, and soccer balls. The other starters made their rounds, too, drawn into conversations and photo ops with girls who wore their numbers and held posters bearing their names or who called out eagerly to them. Jamie had been careful not to encroach on Emma's space. While she didn't necessarily get Emma's paranoia about being seen in public together, she had agreed to respect it, and that meant keeping her distance in front of fans and non-fans alike.

The same went for here in the Gateway Arch, where they were surrounded by mostly tourists, if she had to guess. A handful of people in the lobby had done double takes, and a few others stared at them now, whispering to each other as the group of four women in casual, non-athletic clothes (for once) passed by, one reading determinedly from a Frommer's guide book as the building swayed slightly in the wind.

Jamie itched to take Emma's hand, to place her hand protectively at the base of her spine. Emma always said Jamie's touch soothed her, and Jamie believed her because the same was true for her. But they weren't alone. In fact, that girl on one side of the observation deck was actually taking a picture of them with her phone, if Jamie wasn't mistaken. Possibly a video? Maybe both.

"What year was it built, again?" she asked Emma, relieved when her girlfriend launched into a detailed account of the Arch's construction.

Maddie was right. It did pay to have the nerd squad along.

#

As the game against New Zealand neared, it became even clearer that St. Louis was a Genuine Soccer City. Two days out, Fitzy informed the team that nearly 34,000 tickets had been purchased. That meant the game was on track to sell more tickets than any other standalone friendly in the program's history. A game in Kansas City during the 1999 Victory Tour had sold just over 36,000 tickets, according to the team's history books—and really, did Missourians love soccer that much, or was it that there wasn't anything else to do around here?

"Shut it," Lisa said when Jamie posed this question as they stretched out their legs side-by-side at the end of their next-to-last training session. "I told you they like soccer here. You were just too West Coast biased to believe me."

A shadow passed over them and paused, and Jamie glanced over her shoulder, blinking up at the haloed figure:

Jo.

"Come find me back at the hotel, Maxwell, all right?" she said.

Jamie swallowed hard and nodded, hoping her terror didn't show on her face. "Yes, ma'am."

Jo bit her lip as she turned away, almost as if she was trying not to smile. And, okay, maybe the ma'am had been too much. But Jamie couldn't help being nervous. The coaching staff had been meeting one-on-one with players all week to discuss the World Cup roster, and Jamie was one of the players on the bubble. At some point in the near future—tonight, even?—she was either going to see her dreams once again crushed beneath the USWNT coaching staff's boots, or have her year made. No, her decade. NO, HER CENTURY.

Obviously, she was hoping for the latter.

After dinner, she holed up alone in her room and paced its narrow confines long enough to make it seem like she wasn't desperate to find out what was on Jo's mind. Finally, when she'd deemed enough time had passed—or maybe just when she couldn't take the dread/anticipation another bloody second—she took the hotel stairs three at a time, managing somehow not to trip and break her neck. Jo's room was halfway down the corridor, away from the stairs and elevators, and Jamie jogged toward it, relieved no one else seemed to be around. Once she reached the door, she paused, fist raised to knock.

This is it, she thought. Ellie claimed she had it in the bag, as did Emma. After all, they'd pointed out over dinner, she had started the last three matches. Her spot on the roster had to be secure. But Jamie had had her heart broken too many times to believe in guarantees. Until she knew for sure that she was being offered an official roster spot, she couldn't afford to view her time on the senior team as anything other than temporary. For all she knew, Jo was about to tell her that they'd heard from Steph and she would be back and ready to play for the May friendlies. *Thank you for filling in, but we no longer need your services.*

Jamie didn't really think Jo would say something like that, but at the same time, she couldn't be sure she wouldn't, either.

She took a deep breath, closed her eyes, and repeated her calming mantra: *Om lokah samastah sukhino bhavantu. May all beings everywhere be happy and free.* Including, preferably, her. Ironically, the thing that would make her happiest involved the opposite of freedom: signing her name to a contract that would bind her irrevocably to US Soccer. At least, for an agreed-upon term.

Before one of her teammates could find her standing outside Jo's room on the verge of hyperventilating, she lifted her hand and knocked.

The door opened a moment later, and Jo smiled out at her. Jamie was slightly taller than the national team head coach, which always felt a little odd because that had not been the case the first time they'd met. Back then, Jamie had still been a gangly, awkward teen—a bean pole, according to Emma—not entirely in control of her body. Actually, that was how she felt now as Jo waved her into the hotel suite. Her arms and legs felt jerky and out of synch, and once again she was glad none of her teammates were here to bear witness. The assistant coaches, thankfully, were MIA as well.

"Have a seat," Jo said, waving at the uncomfortable-looking couch in the living area.

Jamie dropped onto one end, and sure enough, it was little better than sitting on a bench. What was it with hotels and their crappy lounge furniture? Maybe they thought their customers would be driven by discomfort to partake of the ludicrously expensive contents of the mini-fridge. Speaking of… She eyed the nearby fridge longingly. She didn't really like beer, but a miniature can of Bud would hit the spot right about now, even if it did cost seven dollars.

"Can I get you something to drink?" Jo asked.

Jamie shook her head quickly and held up her water bottle. "Nope! I'm good." She only just held back the "ma'am" waiting to free itself. Good start.

"So, Jamie, how are you feeling?" Jo asked as she sat down on a nearby armchair. "You haven't had much of a chance to rest lately, have you, given how Arsenal's post-season is going."

"Not really," Jamie admitted, her eyes wandering to the coffee table between them. A folder with her name on it sat just out of reach, and she stared at it briefly before dragging her gaze back to Jo. "But. Yeah. I'm good. Feeling great. Ready to go for sure."

"Glad to hear it. Should we skip the small talk? I feel like maybe we should skip the small talk."

Jamie nodded so quickly she almost made herself dizzy.

"Right." Jo leaned forward and tapped the folder. "First of all, you're getting the start in the six again on Saturday. I believe Mel has mentioned that we're pleased with the way you've stepped up in Steph's absence?"

Jamie nodded again but kept her mouth shut, mildly concerned that something unexpected might emerge if she opened it.

"I spoke with Steph earlier today, and her prognosis is not looking good. Her medical team is giving a best case recovery scenario at eight weeks, which puts us right at the beginning of the World Cup."

"Man, that sucks," Jamie said, disappointed for the veteran star. Steph had come onto the team after the 2004 Olympics, and this summer would likely be her last chance to play in a World Cup. Losing her veteran leadership was a blow that would take time for the team to recover from, too, assuming they even could.

"It does suck," Jo agreed. "Injury is a part of the game, but you hate to see someone go out in a big year. What it means for the team, however, is that a top tier roster spot is coming open."

"It is?" Jamie stared at the coach. They weren't holding Steph's roster spot in the off-chance she would be ready in time?

Jo nodded. "Steph still has a contract with the federation. As I think you know, a player can't be terminated due to injury. However, their contract can be renewed at a lower tier, and that's what's about to happen."

Holy crap. This was huge. The national team had eighteen upper tier and six lower tier roster spots that they reconfigured twice a year. Up until now, Jamie had assumed that the upper tier spots were fixed and that the six lower tier spots were the ones in play for the World Cup roster. But if Steph had been bumped down, who would be bumped up?

Wait. A thought occurred to Jamie, but she pushed it down fast and hard. Nope. Just, nope.

"Steph and I discussed the situation, and do you know what she said?" Jo asked, elbows on her knees as she leaned forward.

Jamie tried to keep her feet on the hotel carpet steady and not jumping all the hell over. "No." *Ma'am.*

"She said we better give you her spot because you're the best thing to happen to the US midfield since she came along."

"I… what?" Jamie stared at Jo, her mouth open.

The coach laughed. "That's exactly how I thought you would react. The staff and I agree with Steph's assessment, which is why we're promoting you. For the next six months, you'll be in position eighteen on the permanent roster. Assuming you want it, of course."

"Want it? Oh my god, of course I want it!" Jamie exclaimed, grinning wide enough to strain her facial muscles.

Jo opened the folder and slid a packet across the table to her. "Normally we wouldn't do things like this, but I know you're leaving for France after the game and I didn't want to have this conversation over the telephone. Also, the timeframe is somewhat constricted given that the NWSL allocation announcement goes out next week. We'll need to have the paperwork squared away by then."

Jamie stared down at the packet, her eyes catching on the US Soccer logo at the top. "So this is really happening? I'm not about to wake up to Britt's impersonation of a diesel engine?"

"This is definitely not a dream. Or, at least, not the kind you wake up from. You've earned this, kiddo. The other coaches and I agree—you're the number six for this team right now. With you on the field, we stand an even better chance at winning this summer. And we already stand a damn good chance."

Reverently, Jamie picked up the stapled sheaf of papers and began leafing through it. Her temporary contract was a page and a half. This contract was significantly longer. She already knew about some of the clauses Emma had to abide by, from social media participation to "lifestyle" rules and requirements. For a moment, Jamie hesitated. Did she really want to sign away her rights to the US Soccer behemoth and become another cog in FIFA's corporate consumption of the beautiful game?

Um, yes. HELL yes.

"It's a lot to take in," Jo said, "so I'm not asking for a decision tonight. You'll need to talk everything over with your rep before you sign. Fitzy says you're working with Joel Rubin's firm?"

Jamie nodded. She'd signed with Sparks Sports Management after the Nike call the previous week and listed them with the federation as her registered intermediary. Ellie had counseled her to let the Sparks folks manage off-the-field business and not let it occupy too much of her brain, but Jamie would be lying if she said she hadn't been losing a perfectly normal amount of sleep over the idea of becoming a Nike-sponsored athlete. This news about her future on the national team should make those negotiations go even more smoothly, she assumed.

She leaned back on the stiff couch as the realization hit her: It was actually happening—she was about to become a US Soccer regular with a Nike contract. All those times her body had betrayed her just as she stood on the brink of realizing her dreams, all those years she'd spent thinking her chances at making the national team were over, finished, kaput, all the tears she'd cried and all the pain she'd gone through were over and done with. Today her story changed.

Today, she belonged.

Barely more than a year ago, she'd been lying on her bed in the house she'd grown up in, nearly despondent over Craig's decision to cut her from the program. She could remember staring up at the glow-in-the-dark constellations she'd picked out as a child and wondering if it might be time to cast her soccer dreams aside. Then fate—and Jo Nichols—had intervened, and Emma and Ellie and Angie and Maddie and Britt and the rest of their friends had stuck by her, and now here she was in a St. Louis hotel on the eve of the World Cup, getting ready to play for her country in front of a crowd of 35,000 Americans as a newly-minted member of the national team's permanent roster.

Or about-to-be-minted, anyway. At this point she didn't even really care about the small print on the contract. She would sign it this minute if Jo asked her to and deal with buyer's remorse later.

Jo's eyes were soft as she watched Jamie. "What do you think, kid? Want me to have Fitzy messenger a copy to Sparks tomorrow?"

"Yes, please," Jamie said. She stood up from the couch, the restless energy swirling through her suddenly too great to resist. "Thank you, Jo. I'm serious. This means so fucking much to me. Oh, sorry." She clapped a hand over her mouth. "Shit—I mean, god, I'm so sorry!"

Jo was laughing as she stood up and stepped around the table, her arms open. "Get in here, Max."

As her coach's arms closed around her, Jamie felt tears pricking her eyes and had to swallow past a growing lump in her throat. This really was it. They really were making her a rostered player on the United States Women's National Team.

Holy crap—she could finally add #USWNT to her Twitter bio.

"Congratulations," Jo said, her voice as firm as her hug. "I can't think of anyone who deserves this more." She pulled away, hands resting on Jamie's shoulders, and looked her in the eye. "I told you I believed you could come out the other side of all of this as a stronger, more focused player, and here you are, Jamie. You did it. This is the culmination of your hard work and your positive attitude. Now, are you ready to go out there tomorrow and show this nation who you are?"

"Yes, ma'am," Jamie said fervently.

Jo smiled and squeezed her shoulders. "Welcome to the show, kid. You deserve it."

"Thanks, Jo."

"You're very welcome. Now, go get some sleep. We need you well rested tomorrow."

"Okay," Jamie said, even though she wasn't sure she would ever be able to sleep again.

"And Jamie," Jo added as she walked her to the door.

"Yeah, Coach?"

"I want you to remember, you earned this. No one is giving you a free pass here. Got it?"

Jamie frowned slightly, unable to fully parse this statement. "Got it."

They slapped hands at the door and Jamie practically floated down the hallway, her momentary confusion already forgotten. She felt buoyant, ecstatic, energized as if she had just scored the game-winner in the World Cup final. Or, you know, what she imagined such a feat would feel like. Maybe if she played well enough, she would actually get a chance to experience that feeling in real life. Now that she was a fully contracted member of the top tier of the US Women's National Team (!!!!!), that was an actual possibility.

She didn't remember running down the stairs to her floor. Suddenly she was just in the corridor, pausing in front of a particular room. She knocked, her knuckles rapping smartly against the surface.

A moment later, it opened to reveal an expectant Emma, still dressed in the shorts and T-shirt she'd worn to dinner. "Well? What did she say?"

"I got the eighteenth roster spot!" Jamie whisper-yelled, grinning as widely as she ever had.

Emma's smile matched hers as she pulled Jamie into a hug, spinning her off the ground and into her room. "I told you it would happen!" As the door closed, she stopped spinning and set Jamie down. "Wait, the eighteenth spot?"

"It was Steph's idea," Ellie said from behind Emma, nudging her out of the way so she could give Jamie an enthusiastic bro hug. "Way to go, Max! I'm so psyched for you. And for the team, of course," she added, winking as she tousled Jamie's hair.

Jamie squirmed away, trying to hold onto a semblance of dignity.

"Steph's not going to be back in time for Canada?" Emma asked, her smile losing a few wattage points.

"No," Jamie confirmed, sobering slightly. "She's eight weeks out at best, Jo said."

"Crap," Emma said.

"I know." As much as Jamie loved getting a spot on the team, she didn't love the idea of Steph losing hers.

"I'm not surprised to hear she supports you, though," Emma added.

"Neither am I," Ellie agreed. "She's one of your biggest fans. I mean, after the two of us, of course."

"Aw, man," Jamie said, ducking her head as she felt her cheeks warm.

Emma and Ellie both laughed at her, and then, before

Jamie could recover, Ellie grabbed her arm and pulled her toward the door. "Come on, Max. Let's go have a captain's meeting. It's a tradition whenever a new player is rostered."

"Oh. Um." Jamie glanced over her shoulder at Emma, who looked as peeved by this turn of events as Jamie felt. "I guess I'll talk to you later?"

Emma nodded. "Yeah. Definitely."

Out in the hallway, Jamie reminded herself that the woman who was waylaying her intended celebration with Emma was an American legend. But soaking in Ellie's presence didn't have quite the same effect it used to. She supposed that happened when you lived in someone's basement.

They were halfway down the corridor when Ellie stopped and smacked her forehead dramatically. "Doh! I forgot, I already have a meeting tonight with Phoebes. One that will take at least an hour, I would think."

"What?"

"I said, I have a meeting that will keep me out of my room for the next hour," Ellie repeated. She winked at Jamie and turned to stroll off down the hall. "See you later, Max."

Plausible deniability, Jamie thought, her natural affection for the national team captain returning in spades. She waited until Ellie had turned a corner and disappeared from view before racing back down the hall and rapping on Emma's door.

"What are you doing he—?"

But Emma didn't get a chance to finish her sentence before Jamie's lips were on hers.

After a moment, Jamie broke away to kick the door shut and make sure it was locked before unsubtly herding

Emma toward her bed.

"We have an hour," she said, tugging at Emma's shirt.

"I love Ellie," Emma said as she obliged, pulling her shirt off over her head.

"Same." Jamie tackled her, laughing, onto the bed. "But I love you more."

"Ditto, nerd."

An hour was an almost luxurious amount of time, Jamie thought as she reached for the clasp on Emma's bra. She damn well intended to make the most of it.

CHAPTER NINE

"All right," Jo said, looking around the locker room. "There's a fantastic crowd out there, as I'm sure we've all noticed. We need to come out of the gates on fire. Be strong and determined in the final third. Let's get lots of goals today."

"Boo-yah!" Phoebe said.

They were standing in their pre-game locker room huddle, arms loose around each other's shoulders, a single moving, breathing entity. The crowd had grown as they warmed up, and now they could hear it like distant thunder overhead, the muffled cacophony of singing, shouting, and banging drums. Emma gripped Maddie's and Gabe's shoulders, trying to ground herself. She shouldn't be so nervous before a friendly. What had her club coach always said was the antidote to nerves? Playing simply and paying attention to the flow of the game. *Back to basics.*

"Use the crowd to your advantage," Ellie added as the coaches and non-starters filed out of the room. "It doesn't get better than this. Use the energy in the stadium, work for each other, and have fun out there. Let's go, let's go, let's go!"

Outside the locker room, the coaching and support staff lined the hallway. The starting players walked the gauntlet, slapping hands and exchanging decisive nods with their coaches. As Ellie had suggested, Emma used the energy in the corridor and beyond to psych herself up, to push down her nervousness, to get herself in the right frame of mind to not only play but to WIN. Win every footrace, win every 50-50 ball, win the freaking game, already.

Play simply and leave it all on the field, she reminded herself as they approached the team of little girls who would stand beside them during the playing of the national anthems. Then they were in the tunnel, listening to the fans only a few feet away, still shouting and singing and stamping their feet. Thirty-five thousand wasn't that much less than the number of people who lived in her Seattle suburb. She took a measured breath, letting the noise wash over her. Ellie was right. The crowd would help them today if they used their energy. The Twelfth Man phenomenon was real—which, as a resident of Seattle, she could attest to.

It helped that the fans in question were knowledgeable about the game. From the signs she'd seen and the songs and chants she'd heard during warm-up, Emma suspected that the people who had shown up this afternoon were not just random soccer aficionados. In fact, she would bet that many of today's ticketholders remembered the late goal against Canada in London three years earlier that had sent the US team to the gold medal match, just as they probably remembered Ellie's last-minute header against Brazil in stoppage time in the 2011 World Cup quarterfinals. What memories would this summer's games provide? It gave Emma chills just to imagine it. But for now, the US needed a good result against New Zealand to demonstrate that the feeling they'd had at residency camp of coming together as a team could translate into on-field success.

Emma smiled down at the little girl standing beside her. She couldn't wait to get out there and freaking START.

At a signal from someone out of sight, the head referee stepped out into the light, her head held high. The US team, led by Phoebe, and the New Zealand team, led by their own captain, followed. The little girl Emma had been paired with squeaked slightly as they emerged onto the field and the sheer size of the crowd became apparent.

Emma squeezed her hand reassuringly and said just loudly enough to be heard, "I like your cleats. Pink is one of my favorite colors, too."

It worked. The little girl beamed up at her as they passed the Fox Sports camera, and Emma smiled back. Then she followed Phoebe, Lisa, and Ryan onto the field for introductions and the playing of both national anthems.

She had played in front of large crowds before, of course. The US had faced Japan in the last World Cup final in front of nearly 50,000 fans, while their rematch a year later at the 2012 Olympics had drawn a record 80,000 spectators to Wembley Stadium. But she'd never seen a crowd like this in the US. At least, not as a player. She'd been lucky enough to attend the '99 World Cup final in Pasadena, where 90,000 other soccer fans had withstood the scorching temperatures and unrelenting sun to cheer on the US women to victory against China.

She wasn't the only one on the current team who had been at the Rose Bowl that day. As the New Zealand anthem droned on, Emma leaned forward and tried to catch Jamie's eye, knowing the cameras would be focused on close-up shots of the other team. Jamie didn't notice at first, but Maddie, who was standing on the other side of Taylor O'Brien, elbowed her. Jamie scowled slightly before following Maddie's line of vision. Then her face cleared and she smiled broadly at Emma.

Their first start together on American soil was happening in front of tens of thousands of screaming Americans. Emma couldn't help but smile back. Then she leaned back into the line and focused on the game again, shaking out her legs to keep her muscles warm and to give her usual pre-game jitters an outlet. Her quads felt a little tired, to be honest. She flushed slightly as she remembered why. Jamie's happiness at being promoted to the regular roster two nights earlier had been prodigious, naturally, and Ellie's decision to absent herself from their room for the hour before curfew had provided ample time to celebrate. Just thinking about it now made Emma's heart rate tick up.

She shook her head and jumped in place, chastising herself for thinking of anything other than the game ahead. But she couldn't help it. Jamie was not only the hottest woman in the national team pool (in Emma's obviously unbiased opinion), she was also an officially rostered player, the starting six, and a soon-to-be Nike athlete.

Life was freaking *good*.

The anthems finally ended, and soon both teams were lining up on their respective ends of the field. Emma squeezed Jamie's shoulder as they passed, careful not to linger too long. She didn't look back, but she could feel Jamie's gaze on her as she joined Phoebe and the other defenders at the top of the box. It was another perfect soccer day, and just as she had against France in the Algarve final, Emma could feel it: They were going to win this game.

The starting whistle finally came, and Emma did her part to execute the coaching staff's strategy. Since Jo had taken over the previous year, she and her assistants had encouraged the players to spread the field, change the point of attack frequently, and maximize flank play. Jo routinely stressed the four Ps of offense: patience, progression, probing, and most of all, possession. On defense she added the fifth and final P: pressure. As soon as they lost the ball, the US players' job was basically to hound the other team until they forced a turnover.

At the Algarve, Jo's tactics had produced obvious returns. As a result, there had been a significant shift in the level of buy-in not only among the press but also among the players. Today would be another test of Jo's full-team attacking mentality—a much more public, heavily viewed test than any of the Algarve games had been. Fortunately, they were up to the challenge. In the 14th minute, capitalizing on a turnover in the New Zealand midfield, Jamie seized the ball and played a give-and-go with Jenny, who slotted a perfect through ball into the box. Emma was already lifting her arms as Jamie took her shot. The ball was still rising when it rocketed into the back of the net, giving Team USA the early lead.

"Hell yeah!" Emma shouted, her voice drowned out by the deafening surge of the home crowd.

Ellie and Jenny reached her first, but Jamie turned in Emma's direction as the other two enveloped her in a bear hug. Emma sprinted up the field to launch herself into Jamie's arms, holding on tightly as their other teammates milled about them. This day really couldn't get any better, she thought, grinning into Jamie's eyes. Which was a sports jinx, but in the best way possible.

"You rock," Emma said over the noise of the cheering crowd.

"Thanks, Em," Jamie said, her eyes conveying her happiness even more than the shit-eating grin occupying her face.

Emma gazed around the stadium as they walked back

to their end of the field, her eyes absorbing the colorful banners and uniforms on display in the stands. It was amazing to feel all the love and support flowing from the fans to the players on the field. She caught Jamie's eye as they got set for New Zealand's kick-off. This was special—not just playing for the USWNT but playing together for their country. This was their mutual childhood dream put into action, and Emma, for one, hoped it wouldn't end anytime soon.

Jamie nodded at her, face solemn now as if she knew exactly what Emma was thinking. Probably, Emma thought as the whistle blew, she did.

The US continued to be dangerous throughout the rest of the first half, but they didn't score again until the 76th minute, when Lisa, the hometown hero, blasted home a pass from Gabe on a short corner. Two minutes later, Emma joined the offense on a free kick and, just as she'd done against France at the Algarve, buried a header on a ball that Jamie placed directly into her path. This time it was Jamie's turn to sprint across the field to congratulate her with a victory hug.

"You're amazing!" Jamie said as she hugged her.

"No, you are!" Emma insisted, laughing.

"For fuck's sake, we all are," Maddie said, crushing them both against her.

Well, Emma thought as they jogged back for another New Zealand kick-off, *we are.*

The final score: 4-0.

After shaking hands and cooling down with the team, Emma and Jamie stuck around with a handful of other players to sign autographs and take selfies with the fans who had come down to field level. They stayed for an extra half hour, soaking up the afternoon sun, chatting with young girls, signing jerseys, and snapping selfies with excited fans beaming the star-struck smile Emma had grown to recognize over the years. At last, one of the national team's interns signaled that it was time to get going, so they waved at the few remaining fans and ducked into the field-level tunnel that led to the locker room. There, they showered and dressed quickly. The rest of the team was probably waiting for them on the bus by now, anxious to get back to the hotel for dinner. The game had started at three, and lunch was a long ways away by now.

As they left the locker room and started making their way through the concrete corridors beneath the stadium, Emma teased Jenny, another of the stragglers, about her lack of offensive fire power on the day.

"Y'all strikers need to get your butts in gear," she said as they neared the stadium exit. "I mean, I don't mind doing your job, but it is a little embarrassing when all the scoring comes from the defense."

The fourth and final goal had come in the 81st minute off a corner kick that had sailed well over the crowd in front of the box. From the opposite wing, Taylor had chipped the ball back in only to have the New Zealand defense clear it. But the clear had lacked power, and Ryan was waiting at the top of the box when the ball rolled toward her on the ground looking for all the world like a perfectly weighted pass. Her low, hard shot had tucked into the left side net, well out of the goalkeeper's reach.

"Whatever," Jenny said now, tossing her long hair still damp from the showers. "I thought we played well as a unit. Besides, you heard Jo. With the World Cup still two months away, we don't want to peak too early."

"Sure, Jan," Emma said, smiling sideways at Jamie as her girlfriend snickered.

Jenny was smiling, too. It would be hard not to, Emma

thought, after a game like today's: perfect weather, a strong showing from every player on the field, and more than the usual appreciation from the stands. Not to mention a more than solid victory. Jo's post-game talk had been encouraging. The team was on the right track, she'd assured them, and at the end of the game, it didn't matter who scored as long as someone did.

They pushed through double doors and emerged into the cavernous underbelly of the stadium, where deliveries of all sorts were made. A few fans with signs and banners stood behind a temporary barrier that stretched between the stadium's interior and the team bus, and Emma briefly admired their fortitude in waiting this long. This would be their last chance to see the team up close. Most of the players would be checking out in the morning and heading back to their club teams for the start of the NWSL season the following weekend. Not Jamie and Britt, though. They would be heading back to Europe for Champions League.

Emma almost wanted to ask Jamie not to go because how awful would it be to finally make the US roster only to get injured playing in Europe? But with the NWSL poised to start its regular season, the risk of injury was the same closer to home. While Jamie was in Europe, Portland would be playing the first three games of the NWSL season, including a match in Chicago.

That was actually better than Seattle's start. Only one of the Reign's three April matches would be played at home. The others would be in Chicago and Kansas City only a couple of weeks before the first World Cup send-off match in San Jose. Emma wasn't looking forward to those turnarounds, either, but it was her job not only to represent her country at the international level but also to further the domestic women's game. That meant giving the pro league her all whenever she could—and, also, stopping to say hello to the fans patiently waiting at the barrier even when all she wanted to do was get on the bus and go back to the hotel.

She was chatting with a young player dressed in her jersey when she noticed Jamie stop halfway to the bus to sign a teenage girl's "Blakewell Lives!" poster. And, seriously? Was Jamie actually trying to break the women's soccer section of the Internet?

At first, Emma didn't notice the dark-haired man skulking behind the teenager and her friends, his pale face glowing in the overhead light. Or, she noticed him, but her eye skipped right over him as Jamie smirked over her shoulder at Emma and motioned her closer to their joint fans. But then the glimpse triggered a red flag somewhere deep inside her brain, and Emma looked back quickly, her amused exasperation at Jamie's recklessness evaporating as the man stepped forward, his eyes on the small group of players signing autographs and chatting with fans. He was looking at the team members as if he knew them, a sly smile turning his plump lips upward as he moved closer.

That was what stood out to Emma—his possessive smile and the rounded softness of his face, his shoulders, his belly under a too-big bomber jacket that shone under the stadium's fluorescent lights.

No, no, no, she thought, dread coiling in her body even as she reached out and tugged Jamie off-balance. It was him. He had found her.

"Get behind me," Emma hissed, her arm slipping around her girlfriend's shoulder as she moved to put herself between the man and Jamie.

"What…?" Jamie blinked at her, confused.

"Finally!" the man said, his voice overly loud and a tad reproachful. "Took you long enough. I've been waiting forever for you girls."

Emma thought about ignoring him and hurrying off to the idling team bus, but the main drive was still 50 feet away, and they couldn't just leave their young fans alone with him. Instead, she tried to remember the training every national team player received at regular intervals: how to de-escalate a potentially dangerous situation. The point wasn't to try to reason with a person who was out of control due to anger or another powerful emotion like obsession. The goal was to reduce the level of agitation as quickly as possible so that a reasonable discussion could take place while you waited for extra help to arrive.

She eyed the man before them carefully. So far, so good. He was smiling and didn't seem particularly agitated. Maybe she was just being paranoid. Maybe he was only a normal fan, and she was blowing his oddness out of proportion because of the proliferation of toxic men on Twitter.

"Hello," she said, assuming a professional smile. "Can we help you with something?"

"Emma..." Jamie's voice trailed off behind her.

Had Jamie been to any of the self-defense trainings? Emma wasn't sure. She glanced over her shoulder. "It's fine, Jamie. I've got this."

"I'm here, Jenny," the man said, ignoring Emma and moving closer to press against the rope barrier. His voice was raised presumably so that Jenny, walking with Maddie and the others just behind Emma and Jamie, would hear him. "Just like I promised."

Jenny. He was here to see Jenny. Emma would forever feel guilty at the relief that washed over her, but she couldn't help it. He wasn't here for her or Jamie. Thank god. *Thank god.*

"I see that," Jenny said, her smile tight as she exchanged a sidelong glance with Maddie. "Thanks for coming. I appreciate the support."

"Well, of course," he said, looking at her as if she was the crazy one. "What kind of man would I be if I didn't come see you play in my city? I'd like to talk to you. Alone," he added, pushing his longish hair out of his eyes and casting a baleful look at the rest of the players as well as at the teenage girls now sidling away, apparently sensing the not-quite-rightness of the exchange.

Out of the corner of her eye, Emma saw Rebecca Perry slip away and head for the bus, her steps unhurried, head down as if she was engrossed by whatever was on her phone. Hopefully she was dialing 911. That was one of the steps in the training: going for help if possible. Speaking of, where was security, anyway? At least he didn't appear to have a weapon, but then again, his loose, shiny jacket could be hiding anything. Meanwhile, Emma's mace was in the bottom of her purse back at the hotel. *Damn it.*

She really hoped she was just being paranoid. Maybe Jenny knew the guy? But a look at her friend's face told Emma everything she needed to know: Jenny was as freaked out as she was.

"Oh, shoot. I wish I could talk to you alone," Jenny said, "but we're not allowed to be in groups of three or less when we're on the road with the team. I can't break the rules or I might not be allowed to play anymore."

"What?" The man looked stricken by the thought. "We can't have that. You're the best striker in the world by far. Although, I guess I might be a little biased as your fiancé, heh heh."

The group stilled. Even Angie, who had quietly been trying to get Maddie to follow Rebecca, froze as the clearly delusional man shrugged and added, "I guess I'll just have to give you this in front of everyone, then." He lifted the rope barrier and ducked under, one hand in his pocket, his eyes intent on Jenny.

The thing about de-escalation tactics, as their most recent trainer at World Cup qualifying had reminded them, was that they were inherently unnatural. Staying calm and detached in the face of possible danger went directly against the human fight or flight reflex. A reflex that people with PTSD, Emma knew, struggled with even on a good day. Just like on the field, she knew what Jamie was going to do before she did it. But Emma's outstretched hand grasped empty air as Jamie moved past her to intercept Jenny's admirer. Emma could only watch helplessly as Jamie almost gracefully shoved the man face first to the ground and sat on him, his arm bent behind his back.

"Ow!" the man cried, struggling against her grip. "You're hurting me! Stop it! *Stop it!*"

"Stay still," Jamie growled, her eyes hard as she held him down.

"Jamie…" Emma said, but then she paused, because they had no idea what the clearly unbalanced man had intended. Maybe he'd wanted to hug or kiss Jenny, or maybe he had a knife up his sleeve or even a gun in his pocket. They didn't know if he was a violent sex offender or a harmless, confused man. For all Emma knew, Jamie had just saved Jenny's life. Or maybe she had escalated the situation unnecessarily. In that moment, there was no way of knowing for certain.

Two things happened at once then: a security guard finally appeared, waving a Taser far too close to Jamie's back, in Emma's opinion, while in the distance, half the players and coaches scrambled off the bus and approached at a run.

"Backup needed at the loading dock," the guard shouted into a mic on his shoulder.

He got his wish sooner than he probably expected as Ellie, Phoebe, and a handful of the others descended on them. Phoebe took Jamie's place, and Emma might have laughed at the absurdly awed look on the stalker fan's face at the switch if she hadn't already felt like crying.

While Phoebe helped the guard secure the man, Ellie tugged Jamie back a few feet. "What were you thinking, Jamie? He could have had a weapon!"

"That's exactly what I was thinking," Jamie replied, her face stonier than Emma had ever seen it.

Emma wanted to add her voice to Ellie's—because now all she could think was that Jamie, the stupid, bloody idiot, had risked herself for Jenny—but instead she finally managed to thaw her body and bowled into Jamie from the side, wrapping herself koala-style around her girlfriend's perfectly intact, perfectly uninjured body.

"Jamie," was all she could say, her voice raw and shaky.

Jamie stared down at her for a moment as if she didn't recognize her. Then she blinked and her arms came around Emma. "Hey," she said, her voice gentling. "Hey, it's okay. It's okay, Em."

"Don't do that," Emma whispered, her voice catching as she hid her face in Jamie's shoulder.

"Don't do what?" Jamie asked, ducking her head to try to get a look at her.

"Don't do that," she repeated, gesturing vaguely at the guy on the ground. "You could have been… Jamie, I can't… You can't just do that!"

Jamie hugged her closer, lips brushing her forehead.

"It's okay," she repeated softly. "We're okay, I promise."

She closed her eyes and buried her face in Jamie's neck, inhaling the scent of her skin, fresh and clean from the stadium's showers. She could have—they might have—*fucking men!* She pulled away and glared at the man on the ground, keeping her arms around Jamie. That son-of-a-bitch. Now she wished she hadn't frozen. Now she wished she had kicked him in the balls or punched him in the head, anything to give the rage inside of her an outlet. Fucking men. Who did they even think they were?

A second guard arrived and Phoebe stepped away so that they could haul the man to his feet. They placed him in handcuffs and read him his rights—which, who knew stadium security had the power to do that—and then they informed him they were going to check him for weapons.

"Why would I have a weapon?" he asked, sounding genuinely confused. "I'm here to see my fiancée. Jenny, tell them!"

Jenny shook her head subtly at the security guards.

"Okay," the first guard said, his voice calmer now that the threat had been averted. "Why don't we go inside and see if we can figure this all out."

The man struggled against the grip of the guards. "But I didn't do anything wrong," he insisted, panting slightly. "That dyke tackled me for no reason! I was just trying to talk to my fiancée and she attacked me!"

Emma turned to face him, keeping her arm around Jamie's waist because, just then, Jo's team time rules could go fuck themselves. The man's hair and clothes were disheveled, and his eyes were wild now, darting back and forth like his brain was short-circuiting. Emma's rage surged again, making her fingertips itch to claw a hole in his face, but she tamped down on the violent urge. The guy was clearly in the midst of a psychotic break, and as such, was he even responsible for his actions? Celebrity Worship Syndrome was an actual obsessive addictive disorder, according to Emma's research. What this man needed was treatment, not verbal assault. So she held her tongue, even though her fight instinct was still flaring up insistently.

A police car pulled up behind the team bus, lights flashing but siren silent. Two police officers emerged and made their way over to the small group. While they conferred with the security guards, Jenny came over to hug Jamie and Emma.

"Thanks, Rook," she said, her smile not quite reaching her eyes. "I appreciate what you did."

"Of course. Are you okay?" Jamie asked.

And that was just like her, Emma thought—more worried about Jenny than herself.

"I'm totally fine. But how are you? You didn't go and get yourself injured, did you?"

Jamie shook her head. "No. I'm fine too."

"I thought for a second Morton there was going to tase you," Jenny said, managing to slip in a reference, Emma noted, to *Twenty-One Jump Street*, one of her favorite movies. Which, hello, this wasn't remotely funny.

"So did I," Jamie said. "I mean, I'm willing to do pretty much anything to win the beep test, but I feel like getting electrically enhanced might be a bit over the top."

"Not to mention, probably ineffective," Jenny agreed.

"Guys," Emma said, pushing their shoulders in turn. "That's not funny!"

"Maybe a little funny," Jenny said, and high-fived Jamie.

Ellie, Phoebe, and Jo were talking to the police. When

the officers moved to escort Jenny's harasser to the squad car parked behind the idling bus, Jo motioned to the players still milling around.

"Let's go," she said. "They want us to head back. An officer will come to the hotel to take your statements after dinner."

Emma looped her arm through Jamie's and tugged her toward the bus, only too happy to leave the creepy underside of the stadium. As the remaining fans dispersed, Emma wondered what kind of stories would show up on the Internet tonight. The whole confrontation had happened so quickly that she doubted anyone had gotten the events on film, but you never knew. Probably it was just as well that the sun was setting and this section of the stadium wasn't very well lit. Even if someone had tried to take pictures or video of the encounter, the resulting images wouldn't be of very high quality. Still, Emma didn't doubt that stories would circulate among USWNT fans on social media. She only hoped Jamie's actions wouldn't attract too much attention.

Actually, she thought as they rode back to the hotel, this was the perfect segue to tell Jamie about her own harassment woes, wasn't it? Compared to Jenny's issues, hers should seem way less worrisome. And now that Jamie had made the roster, Emma didn't have to worry about throwing her off her game. Her reasons for keeping the online harassment to herself were no longer valid. Jamie deserved to know what they were facing, especially if a reprise of tonight's events was a possibility.

Just, maybe she wouldn't tell her tonight, Emma thought, watching Jamie stare out the coach window. Emma could feel the tension emanating from her, could feel the reaction coursing through her as if Jamie's body were her own. Now wasn't the right time to add to her anxiety, and besides, she was leaving for Europe in the morning. Emma would tell her when she got back. *Two weeks*, she promised herself, holding Jamie's hand surreptitiously as the bus navigated the short distance back to the hotel. When they were back in the same country and could see each other for more than a few hours, she would tell her.

Dinner at the hotel was—weird, frankly, with different players stopping by their table throughout the meal to find out exactly what had happened. The collective mood had shifted from relaxed and happy to anxious and jumpy so fast that Emma, for one, was having difficulty processing the change.

A female police officer from the St. Louis Police Department showed up at the end of the meal to meet with those who had been involved in the "incident" and certain members of the support staff, including Jo, Fitzy, Mary Kate, and Caroline, the PR manager.

Emma stayed close to Jamie as they left the conference room where the team dined and headed down the hall to a much smaller room. Maddie and Angie, she noticed, stuck together, too, choosing seats next to each other at the long, oval table.

The officer updated them on Jenny's harasser, providing information on what they had found at his apartment on the outskirts of the city: photos and clippings of Jenny on his bedroom wall and a laptop they intended to search thoroughly. But they hadn't found any weapons at his home, and the only thing they'd found on his person at the time of the encounter was a handwritten note to Jenny in one of his jacket pockets. The district attorney's office had suggested seeking to hold him on criminal stalking charges so that he could receive the mental health help he clearly needed. Either way, he wouldn't be released until after Jenny's flight left in the morning.

As she listened to the officer speak, Emma couldn't help comparing the way the criminal justice system approached a mentally ill white man with how the police in Ferguson, a suburb of St. Louis, had treated Michael Brown, a black man, the previous summer. Not that she wanted anyone to be shot, but still. So much for "blind justice." White men—and women—got the benefit of the doubt even when they didn't deserve it.

"Which one of you is Ms. Maxwell?" the officer asked, glancing around the room.

Jamie held up her hand.

"Right. Can you tell me in your own words what happened at the stadium?"

"Um, sure. We were leaving the locker room—"

"We?" the officer repeated.

Jamie gave her the names of everyone she'd been with after the game—all currently seated at the table—and then resumed her narrative. Her voice was clear as was her memory, and Emma listened intently, impressed by Jamie's steadiness under pressure. The thought occurred to her that she had likely done this before: recited a traumatic event to her parents, her therapist, possibly even a police officer. She probably had more experience with this sort of thing than any of them. At least, as far as Emma knew. Assault was such a private affair, as was harassment. Emma had known that Maddie struggled with online harassment in the past, but they didn't talk about it. Jenny, either, which was why Emma had assumed the deluded man at the stadium was there for her.

After Jamie had finished, the officer asked for confirmation from the rest of the witnesses. They agreed that Jamie's story was accurate, and then the officer turned to Jenny.

"Ms. Latham, is it?"

"That's me," Jenny said, projecting her usual air of positivity blended with mild sarcasm.

"Do you know a Mr. Nathan Butler?"

Jenny's eyes flickered, and when she responded, her voice had lost any trace of flippancy. "*That* was Nate Butler?"

The officer nodded, her eyes sharp on Jenny. "I take it you do know him?"

"I know *of* him," Jenny corrected. She exchanged a look with Caroline, their PR rep, who nodded subtly. "I actually have a dossier I could share with you."

A dossier, Emma thought, her eyes widening.

"A dossier?" the officer repeated.

"It's basically a record of contact with him and some other people online over the past six months. The federation advised me to compile it, so…" Jenny trailed off and flipped her loose hair back over one shoulder, staring almost defiantly at the police officer.

Emma glanced at Caroline, who met her gaze calmly. *Six months.* How many players on this team were tracking their potential stalkers? And why hadn't the federation met with them en masse or offered outside resources? Tonight showed just how vulnerable the members of this team were.

"I see," the officer said, frowning slightly. "And do you have this dossier on hand?"

"No, but I could email you a copy," Jenny said, turning on her phone. "I've got it on Dropbox."

The police officer slid her business card across the table, and while Jenny typed the information into her phone, the officer gazed around the room. "Does anyone else have similar records? We might need them to cross-reference the perpetrator's actions. It's possible Ms. Latham wasn't his only target."

And, *crap*. Emma should have seen this coming. Why hadn't she seen this coming? More importantly, now what? She could lie, but Caroline and Jo would both know she was withholding evidence. There really wasn't a choice, was there?

Lifting her head, she said, "I do," just as Maddie raised her hand.

Emma and Maddie exchanged a startled glance even as Jamie leaned away from the table.

"Are you serious?" she demanded, her eyes on Emma. "Since when?"

Emma gave her a look that she hoped conveyed her sincere apology and her equally heartfelt desire not to have this particular conversation at this exact moment.

"Sorry," the officer said, glancing around the room. "Apparently that was a loaded question."

"It's fine," Jo said. "We just try to keep these things quiet. The players have enough on their plates. The last thing we want to do is spend unnecessary time and energy on off-the-pitch issues. Sometimes, like tonight, it catches up to us."

Her words were as much for the players, Emma knew, as they were for the officer, while her warning look was aimed directly at Jamie. To her credit, Jamie managed to stifle whatever else she wanted to say upon learning that her girlfriend was secretly stockpiling files on an online stalker (stalkers?), but Emma could feel her seething quietly beside her. She'd moved her chair away from Emma's, and as the officer finished taking their statements, Jamie sat stonily, arms folded and mouth pursed in the way Emma had learned to dread.

The officer finally dismissed them with assurances she would be in touch soon. Jamie rose and started toward the door, practically vibrating with angry energy. Before Emma could react, Jo held up a hand.

"Wait a second, guys. Before we release you, I'd like Mary Kate and Caroline to chat with you."

Jamie wavered, and for a moment, Emma thought she might actually stalk out. But Jo was staring at her coolly, eyebrows raised, and Jamie retook her seat, avoiding Emma's entreating gaze.

This, Emma thought, facing front and center again, was exactly why she hadn't told her.

Mary Kate went first, offering up general information about trauma response and suggesting that anyone who might need help processing what had happened earlier should stop by her room later. She would be happy to talk, any time of the day or night. They didn't even need to call first.

Caroline, the team's PR rep, went next. Basically, she explained, they weren't to discuss the incident with anyone outside the team. Not with friends or family and especially not with members of the press. This was not the type of subject the US national team discussed in public forums. Emma had expected this, but as Caroline finished issuing her directive, she wondered again if there was video evidence of the incident already floating around the World Wild Web, as Maddie sometimes called it.

Maddie, who had a dossier like hers, as did Jenny.

Why hadn't they talked about that fact? Probably because her friends, like Emma, had been cautioned to keep their situation quiet. Couldn't let anything besmirch

The Road to Canada

the federation's reputation, could they? Or maybe that wasn't fair. In their meeting in LA, Caroline had suggested that online harassers were attention seekers, and the best way to defuse their fixation was to deny them what they were looking for. Emma didn't believe it was that simple, but she did come from a long line of Scandinavian Minnesotans who believed that ignoring unpleasant emotions just might make them go away. Jamie, on the other hand, raised in crunchy Northern California, was more of a processor. This could be both a blessing and a curse, Emma had come to realize.

As soon as Jo released them, Jamie was out the door, her shoulders tense and jaw set. Emma followed her, aware of Maddie and Angie watching sympathetically. This is what they got for inter-team dating, she could almost hear Jenny thinking at her. Loudly.

In the lobby, Jamie veered toward the hotel entrance, her movements short and choppy. Emma followed her outside onto the hotel's curved drive, trying to decide if she should give her space. But a car was pulling up and the concierge nearly bowled Jamie over, and *Jesus*, she was going to get herself hurt.

"Jamie, wait!"

Jamie's brow furrowed as she glanced over her shoulder. "Leave it, Emma."

"I can't," she said. "It's not safe."

This part of downtown St. Louis, only steps from the Mississippi River, was an odd mix of parking lots, hotels, and reclaimed factory spaces. Despite the fact they were staying at a luxury hotel attached to a popular casino, Fitzy had informed them when they arrived that the neighborhood was not one to get lost in after dark.

Jamie glanced away, still frowning. "I need some air."

"I get that, but don't walk away mad. Come back inside. Please?"

Another long moment passed during which Emma contemplated using her slight advantage in weight and upper body strength to keep Jamie from storming off. Then Jamie nodded jerkily. "Fine."

She turned and followed Emma back into the building, not saying a word as they walked to the elevator. Only when Emma pressed the button for the eighth floor did Jamie turn toward her, frowning again. "What are you doing?"

"You said you needed air," Emma explained, leaning against the back of the elevator, hands folded behind her. "Personally, I could use a drink. It's not every day someone on the team gets attacked by a delusional fan."

At that, Jamie's shoulders slumped. "Emma…" she said, her voice low.

"Yeah?" she asked, hope—the annoying pest—flaring inside. Maybe this would be okay. Maybe *they* would be okay.

But Jamie only shook her head and watched the numbered floors change in silence.

On a Sunday night in April, the hotel's rooftop restaurant wasn't busy. At the entrance, Emma stopped and exchanged a few words with the host, who glanced between her and Jamie and nodded, her eyes curious. Emma touched Jamie's arm and led her outside to the part of the patio where an upscale bonfire/fountain combo created both warmth and soothing sounds. A pair of curved wicker chairs with thick cushions sat empty in a corner, and Emma nodded in their direction.

"Will you sit with me? Please? I really think we should talk about this."

"Now you want to talk about it?" Jamie's tone was more than a little bitter. Still, she let Emma guide her to the corner where a stone wall topped with low bushes provided a sense of privacy without hiding the view of the nearby Gateway Arch and the city's assortment of taller buildings, all lit up against the evening sky.

"Thank you for not leaving," Emma said, depositing her purse on a low coffee table.

Jamie dropped onto the other chair and folded her arms across her chest. "You're welcome," she said, her tone grudging at best.

"I'm sorry," she offered, fidgeting at the edge of her seat.

"You're sorry," Jamie repeated, her tone still edged with antagonism.

"I am. Truly."

"About lying to me? Or about getting caught?"

"That's not fair," she said, sitting up straighter on the absurdly comfortable patio chair.

"Isn't it, though?"

Emma was still cycling through responses in her mind when an aproned server appeared with schooner-sized glasses of beer, a plate of french fries, and dark red cloth napkins that matched his apron.

"Here you go," he said, smiling as he deposited the food and drinks on the coffee table. "Enjoy."

"Thanks," Emma said, and reached for her beer. She took a long pull, grateful to have something to do with her hands. Then she noticed Jamie wasn't drinking. "It's a lager shanty, if that helps."

As the scent of fried food wafted between them, Jamie's stubborn expression relaxed slightly and she leaned forward, delicately rescuing a single fry from the pile. She dipped it into the spicy house ketchup and lifted it to her mouth almost reluctantly. But after she'd chewed and swallowed, her lips turned up. Infinitesimally, but Emma saw it. French fries were Jamie's weakness. She didn't let herself indulge often, a fact that Emma wasn't above exploiting.

"Now who's not being fair," Jamie grumbled, her eyes on the plate as she went back for more.

Emma considered saying that she had never claimed to play fair but decided that was probably not the best line to go with, considering. Instead, she helped herself to a handful of the fried potato goodness. Rattled by the afternoon's events, she hadn't eaten as much at dinner as she normally did after a game, and now her calorie-deprived body was communicating its displeasure. Judging from how rapidly the plate of french fries disappeared, Jamie's body was staging a similar revolt.

They had barely finished wiping the salt from their fingers when their server appeared beside them. "Another order of fries? Or would you like me to bring you a menu?"

Emma looked at Jamie, her eyebrows lifted.

"More fries, please," Jamie said, only slightly less grudgingly. Then she added politely, "Thank you."

As the server whisked the empty plate away, Emma leaned back in her chair, toying with the cloth napkin in her lap. Jamie was sticking around for at least as long as it took to demolish another plate of fries. Right. She could work with that.

"I'm sorry for keeping my online situation a secret," she said before the silence could settle too heavily between them.

"It isn't exactly a secret, though, is it?" Jamie asked, face closing again as she refolded her arms across her chest. "I mean, the staff obviously knows. That's what all the meetings have been about, haven't they?"

Emma took a breath, willing herself not to respond to the obvious aggression in Jamie's tone. She glanced up at the sky, but there were no stars to be seen. She wasn't sure if that was because the sun hadn't been down for long or because the city's light pollution blocked out the constellations. Maybe both.

"I know you're upset, and I understand why," Emma said, trying to keep her tone even. "But what was I supposed to do?"

"Are you serious? What were you supposed to do?" Jamie repeated, her tone disbelieving. "You were supposed to freaking communicate with me, Emma, not let me get blindsided by someone else."

"I didn't want my baggage to be a burden for you when you were trying to make the roster. Why is that so terrible?"

"It's so terrible," Jamie said, "because you lied to me. For months! Again."

"Again?" Emma shook her head. "What are you even talking about?" But as Jamie continued to stare at her, one eyebrow lifted in challenge, Emma remembered: Tori Parker. Her lie of omission regarding the former youth pool player was why Jamie had stopped talking to her the first time. *The first time.* A chill settled over Emma that had nothing to do with the cool spring night. That wasn't actually—Jamie wouldn't do that again. She wouldn't summarily cut Emma out of her life over this, would she?

Jamie shook her head. "I don't understand why it's so hard for you to be honest, Emma. What is it, like, a congenital defect you inherited from your father?"

"Actually, behavior is learned, not inherited," Emma shot back before she could stop herself.

Jamie's lips parted no doubt to release another well-placed barb, but she didn't get a chance as their server appeared and slid another plate of steaming fries between them.

"All set for now?" the man asked, already backing away.

This time, Emma only nodded, not trusting her voice.

Silence descended again as they devoured the food in the same ruthless, efficient fashion as before. When they were done, Jamie wiped her mouth with her napkin and stared at Emma across the low glass table. "I have a question. Has what happened to Jenny ever happened to you?"

Emma hesitated only briefly before shaking her head. Despite the threats over the years, no one had ever shown up in person at a team event or, worse, her home. Not that she knew of, anyway.

"Are you sure? Because you don't seem so sure," Jamie said, her voice biting.

"No, I'm sure." Emma wished she could rewind. Why was it she never seemed to say the right thing when someone was angry with her? "I've never had anyone approach me in person. It's only been online."

"How long has it been going on?"

Emma paused. "Do you mean recently, or in general?"

"What do you mean, in general?" Suddenly Jamie's gaze sharpened. "Oh my god. This is the thing your brother was talking about, isn't it?"

Freaking Tyler. Why had he opened his big mouth? "I

was going to talk to you about all of this after Champions League—"

Jamie cut her off, scoffing. "Of course you were, Emma. Totally believable."

"I really was. I was just waiting until you heard about the roster, and then I didn't think it was the best topic to bring up right before you flew back to Europe." *Right before you flew back to France*, she really meant, but she was fairly certain she didn't have to make that distinction obvious.

Jamie gazed at her a second longer, her lips pursed in that way that variously signaled anger, fear, hurt, or any combination thereof, before she balled up her napkin and deposited it on the coffee table. "If that's it," she said, her voice hard as she rose to tower over Emma, "I guess I'll see you when I see you."

What? What did that even mean? Emma stared up at her. She wanted to tell Jamie to grow the fuck up. She wanted to ask if they were breaking up. She wanted to beg Jamie not to go, not to leave her alone. She wasn't sure she could take being left—*again, god damn it*—by her. What kind of tattoo would she mark her body with this time? An arch to signify the setting of their final meal together?

But it wouldn't be their last meal together. Jamie had made the roster, which meant they had many, many more shared meals to look forward to in their future.

Fuck, *fuck*, FUCK. This was exactly what Emma had worried would happen before she and Jamie had started dating. And it was all her fault, once again. Jesus, she was such a mess. Jamie would be better off without her, just like Sam was. Emma had heard through the lesbian sports professional grapevine that Sam was engaged to her field hockey coach girlfriend. More power to them both.

"Fine," she said after a long moment. She leaned

forward and reached for her purse. "See you when I see you." She pulled out her credit card and glanced around, looking for their server.

Jamie pulled a few bills from the pocket of her team sweats and flung them onto the table. "I've got the tip."

"You don't have to do that. I'm the one who dragged you out here."

"It's fine, Emma." She grabbed her schooner glass and gulped down its contents. "I'm out."

"Fine," Emma echoed. She held her own glass between her palms, the heat of the bonfire at her back, the Gateway Arch lit up before her. And then: "Safe travels," she added, because she couldn't not say it. Jamie would be flying across the Atlantic twice in the next week, not to mention crossing the English Channel. Even if they were breaking up, Emma still had Jamie's itinerary in her email. She would still be checking her flight status tomorrow to make sure she'd arrived in London, would still be following Arsenal's progress in its two semifinal legs against Lyon, would still be setting an alert on her phone for when Jamie's return flight to Portland was supposed to land. Even if Jamie wanted nothing more to do with her, Emma couldn't stop caring just like that.

She felt rather than saw Jamie pause beside her, heard the soft sigh fall from her lips. "Safe travels to you, too," Jamie said, her voice low. "I'll call you when I get back from France." And then the familiar heat of her beautiful body shifted closer, and Emma's eyes drifted shut as Jamie's lips brushed her hairline, her touch as light as a ghost's.

In the next moment she was gone, her warmth replaced by the weak gusts of heat from the gas bonfire. Emma lifted her glass of beer and drank deeply, her eyes on the Arch. The architect responsible for the design had died before the metal and glass behemoth could be completed, she'd read in the guide book. He'd only been 51—two years older than her father when he died. Her dad had come to St. Louis more than a handful of times to ply his surgical technique. Had he stayed at this very hotel? He must have looked out over a similar view, anyway. Had he missed her and Ty and their mom? Or had he been only too happy to take a break from the family life he'd seemed increasingly a peripheral part of by the end? Maybe his girlfriend—that woman, as Emma still thought of her—had flown out to meet him, and they'd enjoyed a romantic St. Louis getaway.

Yeah, no. Emma barely considered this possibility before rejecting it. Her father had traveled to far more interesting locales than the gateway to the American West. It seemed more likely that his girlfriend had met him in New York or LA for a weekend of—Emma stopped the thought, wrinkling her nose. Way too much information.

Was lying in fact a behavior she'd learned at her father's knee? She supposed it was possible. She lifted her nearly empty glass to the grayish brown sky. "Thanks, Dad. Honestly." And then she laughed—if you could call it that—at her own word choice.

The server appeared at her side again, his smile sympathetic as he touched Emma's credit card, still lying face up on the table. "Is that it, or can I get you anything else?"

"Another beer would be good, actually," Emma said, tapping her glass. "Only, make it a pint this time?"

"Of course," the man said, nodding.

Emma sat back in her chair, arms folded across her body, and watched a helicopter blink its way along the twists and turns of the Mississippi River. Tomorrow night at this time, she would be watching a similar scene play out over the Space Needle and Puget Sound. And Jamie, where would she be? Crashing at Allie's cousin's flat in Camden, where Emma had surprised her five months earlier on the spur-of-the-moment trip that still stood out as the best vacation ever.

Would it be their last vacation ever? Emma closed her eyes and prayed to the god she didn't actually believe in.

"Your pint," the server said, his voice apologetic.

Emma opened her eyes. "Right. Thanks."

Time to get her shit together. Or, actually, it was time to drink this delicious pint. There would be plenty of time later to get her shit together, assuming the zombie apocalypse didn't get her first.

"Modern humans have been around for tens of thousands of years," Jamie pointed out whenever Emma joked darkly about the impending apocalypse. "How unlucky would we have to be to be alive at the end of the world?"

"Well, someone has to be alive for it," Emma usually replied. "Why not us?"

Why not them, indeed. At least as residents of urban areas they would probably fall in the first wave. That meant they wouldn't survive to fight their way through a nightmarish landscape to questionable safety. Of course, it also meant they wouldn't be together at the end, since Jamie had turned down Emma's invitation to move in with her.

Nope. Not going to think about that, Emma told herself. Back to the zombie apocalypse. Or maybe the inevitable alien invasion. Because with 100 billion known galaxies and more being discovered every day, it seemed impossible that there wasn't alien life out there *somewhere*, waiting to descend on their beautiful blue-green planet and steal it out from under them the way Europeans had snatched North America from its indigenous population. With human-induced climate change going the way it was, though, there might not be much left soon for any erstwhile alien invaders.

At the edge of the Mississippi River in the shadow of the Gateway Arch, Emma drank her pint and plotted the course of her fate at the end of the world—anything other than thinking about the feel of Jamie's lips against her forehead not knowing if that was the last time Jamie Maxwell would ever kiss her.

CHAPTER TEN

Jamie sat at her gate, sipping green tea and watching the sparse pedestrian traffic pass as she waited for boarding to begin. Even the flight crew that had wheeled their baggage through the door and onto the jet bridge had looked only half-awake. Which, while understandable given the ridiculously early hour, did not inspire confidence.

Frowning slightly, she checked her phone screen, but it remained blank. She and Britt had left the hotel at half past four that morning without seeing anyone else from the team. They were the only ones headed overseas—London by way of O'Hare—thus the early departure time. Nearby, Britt was calling her family to tell them she loved them. Jamie couldn't count how many times she had watched Britt go through this pre-travel ritual. The St. Louis airport was one of the smaller ones they had flown through, with no club lounge even in the international terminal. The building design here was the same as in the domestic terminal, with arches and domes that reflected the city's style. She glanced up at the nearest arch, awash with colored lights, and blinked as her conversation with Emma on the hotel terrace the previous evening came back to her.

Emma. Jamie still couldn't quite believe that Emma had kept something so major from her. Except that wasn't entirely true. She'd known Emma was hiding something, had even assured her that it was fine for her to keep parts of her life private. In a way, she'd enabled Emma's lying, which—*fool me once, shame on you; fool me twice…* But in her defense, she had thought Emma wanted to keep her past private, not her present.

She checked her phone again, wondering if Emma would break the radio silence Jamie had imposed. Nothing yet. Emma's flight didn't leave for a little while, though, so there was still time. If this were a romantic comedy, Emma would come sprinting down the corridor just as Jamie was about to board. With visions of *Love, Actually* dancing through her head, Jamie couldn't stop herself from glancing at the corridor every so often as the crew readied their plane for take-off. She couldn't deny, either, the surge of disappointment that swept through her chest when she boarded the airplane, nor the realization that swept over her as the flight crew sealed the airplane door and the aircraft began to back away from the gate: Emma really wasn't coming after her.

Then again, it wasn't really up to Emma to come after her, was it? Jamie was the one who had said they shouldn't talk until after she got back. She was the one who had walked away. If she were being honest, she had always been the one to walk away, and not just from Emma, either. She had left every major and most of the minor relationships she'd ever had, starting with her high school girlfriends, none of whom she'd dated for long. Was that just who she was? When things got difficult, did she shut off and look for the nearest exit? Shoshana, her therapist in Berkeley, said her "strong self-protective instinct" was healthy, but to Jamie (and probably to the girls and women she'd dated), her reactions didn't always seem that commendable.

Not that she was the only one with issues. Emma struggled with being open and honest. She always had and maybe she always would. Jamie remembered something her sister had said shortly before marrying Todd: She didn't need him to be perfect. He'd made numerous mistakes in their relationship, as had Meg, and she fully expected the blunders to continue. The reason she was marrying him was that she had decided she could live with his particular imperfections. She could see a viable, long-term future with him despite his flaws, and, in fact, wanted that future very much. Todd, in turn, had decided he could accept her "quirks," as Meg called them, if it meant he got to plan a life with her.

The question here, Jamie thought as the airplane lumbered into the air and angled itself away from St. Louis, was whether or not she could accept Emma's propensity to keep secrets. Or if, possibly, Emma could learn to mitigate those tendencies and approach Jamie with a more open head and heart. That last part wasn't up to Jamie, though. Only Emma could make that kind of change—assuming she wanted to.

While Britt watched the earth fall away beyond the window, murmuring her usual quiet prayer, Jamie leaned her head back against her seat. This was not how she'd expected this trip to begin. She'd made the permanent roster, for Christ's sake! She was going to play in the World Cup in a matter of weeks! She should be bouncing off the plane's heavily reinforced walls. But instead, she couldn't stop replaying the previous day's events in slow motion: how Emma had put herself between Jamie and the man she'd only just noticed was not entirely stable; how Jenny's delusional stalker had stepped under the rope barrier, misplaced entitlement oozing from every pore; how an uncontrollable wave of rage had surged through Jamie, catapulting her into thoughtless action that had ended with him on the ground beneath her, crying out in fear. In that moment, some part of her had delighted in his pain. A cruel voice inside her head had goaded her to press his face harder into the concrete, to twist his arm until it snapped. If the security guard hadn't come running when he did, she honestly wasn't sure what she might have done.

Afterward, on the bus, she'd felt sickened by her own cruelty. He hadn't been carrying a weapon, the police officer had told them at the meeting. He genuinely believed that he was engaged to Jenny and couldn't understand why she had denied their relationship. He was clearly mentally ill and, as the officer had said, desperately needed help. Jamie had sat in that conference room feeling guiltier and guiltier—until the moment when the earth shifted beneath her because as it turned out, Emma had been keeping a dossier on various online stalkers for months now. Maddie was also keeping files on her harassers, a fact that Angie had chosen to keep from Jamie, too.

And why was that? Why did everyone keep hiding important shit from her?

This was exactly what Jamie had asked Angie the night before when she'd dropped by her room after leaving Emma at the rooftop restaurant.

Angie had looked at her, frowning, and said, "You know why. We love you, Max. Of course we're not going to tell you about this crap."

Jamie had stared at her, mind whirling. Had Emma told Maddie who in turn had told Angie about France? Or maybe Britt, one of the only people Jamie had ever confided in about the assault, had told Angie years ago. Who else knew? Did everyone on the team know? Did they freaking talk about what had happened to her when she wasn't around?

But then Angie had interrupted her spiraling to add, "We've all been on the bubble, Jamie, and we know it's not an easy place to be. I didn't want to do anything to risk messing with your focus. Can you really say you wouldn't have done the same for me?"

And no, Jamie had realized. She couldn't say that at all.

As it turned out, Maddie hadn't told Angie about the dossier right away, either. She'd hidden it until Angie intercepted a text from one of Maddie's sisters that referenced her "online situation."

"I was pissed at first that she kept it from me, too," Angie had said as they lounged on her bed, a muted baseball game playing on the nearby television. "But I get why."

Jamie had frowned. "You do?"

"Yeah. We try to keep the off-the-field stuff compartmentalized, you know? Otherwise it would spill over onto the field, and neither of us wants that. Anyway, you can't control other people. It's a waste of time and energy to try."

Some of the "off-the-field stuff" she was referring to, Jamie knew, was their families' objections to their relationship. Neither the Wangs in New Jersey nor the Novaks in Illinois were enamored of their daughters' romantic involvement. Fortunately, as the happy couple had pointed out numerous times, their duty to club and country meant they saw each other significantly more than they saw their families.

As the plane levelled off at cruising altitude, Britt glanced away from the window. "Oh, good. They're starting the beverage service. You still up for a mimosa?"

Britt had found out even before Jamie that she was

being offered a roster spot for the World Cup. Trish Bailey, one of Phoebe's back-ups, had retired suddenly a few weeks earlier. Britt had already been outpacing the older woman, but now the way forward was clear. Britt and Jamie would both be going to the World Cup—barring catastrophic injury in the next eight weeks, of course.

Amazing what a difference a year could make.

"I don't know," Jamie hedged, remembering her panic attack a year and a half earlier after imbibing too much wine at a team dinner. The last thing she needed right now was to lose control over her emotions and end up getting kicked off the plane in Chicago. That would definitely be a violation of the professionalism clause of her as-yet unsigned federation contract.

Beside her, Britt turned in her seat and touched her arm. "Are you okay? You seem quieter than usual."

Jamie shrugged. "It's just really early." Britt was so excited about the roster news, and they would be traveling for the next eleven hours. It wasn't like Jamie could do anything about her situation with Emma anytime soon, even if she'd wanted to.

But her friend persisted. "Come on, little buddy. What's up? I thought it was just your usual morning mood, but there's something else going on, isn't there?"

Jamie stared at her, semi-offended. "Excuse you. I am a morning person by nature."

Britt snickered. "Yeah, right. Whatever you say, James."

"Jackass." Jamie huffed and folded her arms across her chest. Then she unclenched her fists and forced the rest of her body to relax, too. The defensive posture was becoming way too familiar, as was its chemical influence on her brain.

"Seriously, is this about what happened at the stadium?" Britt asked.

"No. Well, in a way, I guess. It's Emma, actually."

"Ah. I wondered why you guys didn't talk before take-off."

While Britt called everyone she loved before boarding an airplane because the ritual assured the superstitious portion of her mind that nothing bad would happen, Jamie's friends on the team knew that she and Emma talked before flying because of Emma's fears, not hers.

"So what's up?" Britt prodded. "You and Emma seemed pretty tight right after everything went down."

"We were, at first. But now, well, I guess we're sort of taking a break?" As Britt's mouth dropped open, Jamie hurried to add, "Not that sort of—not like a Ross and Rachel break. Or, I guess, a Rachel break but not a Ross one? We're just taking some space. I said I'd call her when I get back to Portland, that's all."

Britt was still staring at her. "That's more than a week away!"

"I know," Jamie said, and sighed as she pictured the Emma-less days stretching away in front of her. Seriously, what had she been thinking? Except she hadn't been thinking, obviously. She'd been too busy fighting and flighting.

"Is she pissed at you for tackling that guy yesterday?" Britt asked. "Because that seems a little hypocritical, given the whole Rocky incident."

"No, it isn't anything like that." Now that Jamie knew what Emma had been dealing with off the pitch, her reaction the day they'd scrimmaged the boys' team actually made a lot more sense.

"Then what is it?" Britt asked. "I thought you guys were doing really well."

"We were." Jamie hesitated, and then as her best friend since college continued gazing earnestly at her, she found herself spilling the details of the meeting with the police officer and her conversation with Emma at the hotel restaurant.

"Their fries really are awesome," Britt said, momentarily sidetracked by the mention of food.

"I know. I think it's the seasoning."

"Totally." Britt's dreamy gaze gave way to a sympathetic glance. "So you cut and ran, huh?"

"I didn't—" Jamie started to protest. But then she stopped and glanced down at her hands, tangled together in her hoodie's center pocket. "Seems to be a hard habit to shake."

"Um, the lyrics are 'a hard habit to break,'" Britt corrected her.

After living with Britt on and off for nearly a decade, Jamie was well-acquainted with the keeper's outsized enthusiasm for the musical stylings of Chicago in general and Peter Cetera in particular. It was really too bad you could find almost anything on digital these days.

"My bad," Jamie dead-panned, and then elbowed her friend. "Goof."

"Butthead. Seriously, I wouldn't worry about taking off on her. It's not like you had a choice," she said, gesturing around the airplane's interior.

Jamie rolled her eyes at the pun.

"No, really," Britt insisted. "I'm sure Emma understands you need some space after what happened. I mean, she did lie to you, by her own admission. But maybe don't wait until you're back in Portland to get in touch with her, especially if you're worried about the whole cutting and running thing."

"What do I say to her, though? 'Hey, I know I said I would call you when I got home, but surprise, I decided I wanted to talk to you sooner?'"

Britt shrugged. "Why not? I think you're overthinking this, Max. You guys are a couple, and that means you're going to have problems. Everyone does."

"Even you and Allie?"

"Of course we do. She makes me sleep on the couch probably once a week on average—and not because I snore."

Jamie tilted her head doubtfully because that didn't seem right.

"Okay, I'm sure she's glad I'm down the hall because of the snoring," Britt allowed, "but you know that a couple of thin walls don't muffle the sound that much."

Yes, indeed, Jamie did know that. "When's your apnea appointment, again?"

"When we get back."

"What kind of testing will they make you do?"

Britt eyed her. "Are we really changing the subject now?"

"I think so. Thanks for listening, though. I appreciate it."

"Anytime, little buddy," Britt said, and tugged Jamie closer to place a resounding kiss on the top of her head.

Sometimes Jamie forgot how tall her best friend really was.

"But screw sleep apnea," Britt added, starting to

bounce in her seat. "Can we please drink booze and talk about the World Cup? You know, the one that we're both going to as ACTUAL PLAYERS?"

Jamie laughed and nodded. One mimosa wouldn't hurt.

#

At half past one a.m. London time, as she and Britt peeled themselves out of the cab and hoofed their way into Allie's cousin Lizzie's flat, Jamie reflected that one mimosa definitely wouldn't have hurt. But when their seatmate on the Chicago to London leg overheard them talking about their summer plans, one drink somehow became three on a stomach only partially filled with airline food. In an unfortunate mirroring of her return trip from Lyon a decade earlier, Jamie very nearly ended up vomiting in a tiny airplane lavatory halfway over the Atlantic. Fortunately, she'd managed to keep her unhappy stomach semi-appeased by taking a fitful nap the last third of the flight, but now as they dropped their things on the floor and crawled into the guest room double, the world felt like it was shaking again and she cursed the lack of a self-protective instinct where mimosas on airplanes were concerned.

And yet, her body still felt like it was early evening. Despite the fact she'd been up at four that morning, she wasn't sleepy. She just felt shitty, thanks to the alcohol still poisoning her bloodstream. Why did drinking always seem like a good idea at the time, even when she knew—*she bloody knew*—it definitely was not? She pulled out her phone, as she'd been doing ever since they'd landed, and checked her messages. Nothing from Emma. She read through their text thread, full of photos and hearts and easy declarations of love, smiling to herself here and there at Emma's incredibly dorky adorableness.

She scrolled back down and stared at the last message Emma had sent her, the night before the game: "I AM SO PROUD OF YOU!! And, plus, I really really love you." The text was followed by a string of GIFs and emojis, including an animation of the 2015 Canada World Cup mascot, a great white owl, preening with a gold medal around its neck. Seriously, where had Emma even found that?

Jamie hesitated, and then she typed, "Got to Lizzie's a little while ago. Now trying to sleep off mimosas with Britt. Remind me never to drink on a plane again." She paused, and then added, "Sorry about last night. Love you." And then, before she could rethink it, she hit send.

Not even thirty seconds passed before Emma's return came winging across the entirety of North America and the Atlantic Ocean: "Thanks for letting me know!! I'm home as well. And *I'm* sorry about last night… I love you too. Talk soon?"

"Absolutely," she typed. "Call you after dinner tomorrow?" That was the time they'd picked the previous month when she was in Europe and Emma was in Seattle.

"I would love that," Emma wrote back, "but I also understand if you need time and space to think."

Jamie bit her lip, staring at the words. She was in Europe and Emma was in Seattle for the next ten days. Shouldn't that be more than enough time and space to process? Besides, what had Jo said right before the Algarve championship? The simple brilliance had stuck with Jamie: *In sport as in life, there is no looking back, only moving forward.* She'd also said, scarily appropriate to Jamie's life, "Leave what happened in France where it belongs: in France." But that was for a different conversation.

"We obviously need to talk when I get back," she replied, "but I do understand why you did what you did, even if I don't like it. Okay?"

"Okay," came the lightning-fast reply. "Thank you, Jamie."

"No—thank YOU," she wrote back, adding a cheesy wink for good measure.

"Dork."

"Nerd."

"Now drink some water and get to sleep," Emma ordered.

"Yes, ma'am," Jamie wrote back, wondering where her water bottle was but too sick to go looking.

"Sweet dreams, Jamie. I miss you."

"Miss you too," she answered, adding a few heart emojis. And then: "Sweet dreams to you too."

Not that Jamie would be sleeping anytime soon. As she turned off her phone and rolled over, Britt's snores resounded through the room. Jesus Christ on a pogo stick, how did Allie ever get any sleep? That apnea test couldn't come soon enough, as far as Jamie was concerned.

She readjusted her travel ear plugs, closed her eyes against the London street lights leeching through the blinds, and waited without much hope for sleep to find her.

#

Fortunately, the first leg of the semifinals was in London. That gave Jamie a chance to reacclimate herself to Europe before having to face Lyon. Not that she and Britt had been away from Europe for long. As they visited old friends and old haunts in London, her favorite city ever—other than San Francisco—she was glad for the oddly relaxing week in the UK. Her contract was signed and sorted, the World Cup roster set, and the Nike deal settled thanks to Amanda, her new agent at Sparks Sports Management. Things were moving along nicely. Better than nicely—TREMENDOUSLY.

The federation made the roster announcement official on April 14, the day after Arsenal lost to Lyon 2-1 in the first leg of the semis. She and Britt read it together on Britt's cousin's laptop, and seeing her name in print made her selection real in a way she hadn't expected. She turned to Britt and found that her friend's eyes were tearing up, too.

"We made it!" Jamie said, grinning at her.

"We totally did," Britt said, sounding just as astounded as Jamie felt as she pulled her into a bear hug. "Holy shit, James! We're going to the show!"

Thank god Britt was there. Otherwise, Jamie might have felt lonely and far from home as the calls and text messages blew up her phone. But with her best soccer friend in the world at her side, it was impossible to feel anything other than excited.

That night, they celebrated at the pub with the team, a few others of whom had their own World Cup roster selections to drink to, and it was just like the old days. Except that Allie was back in DC, and Clare was with someone new, and Jamie—Jamie was in love with Emma Blakeley, who had lied to her about something important. The more things changed… Except things had changed. Really.

No looking back, she reminded herself as she sipped her lager shanty and laughed at one of her teammate's bad jokes. Only moving forward.

A few days later, Jamie was again glad to have Britt by her side as the team coach passed through the outskirts of Lyon, headed for the stadium on the south side of the city.

And yet, a decently-sized part of her was disappointed when they arrived at the hotel in Lyon and Emma wasn't there. That shouldn't have been a surprise. The Reign had played in Chicago the previous day, and Jamie and Britt had watched the match on YouTube. It made perfect sense that Emma wasn't here, Jamie told herself as she changed into practice gear in the hotel that was spitting distance from Lyon's stadium and walked with the rest of the team to their afternoon training session. She had probably been silly to even hold out a frisson of hope.

At the stadium, Britt typed a quick text into her phone and then threw it into her bag. "Have a good practice, James," she said with a secret smile as she turned away to join the other goalkeeper for warm-up.

And there. What was that? Jamie narrowed her eyes at her best friend.

"Anytime, Maxwell," their young Irish assistant coach barked.

Right. Head in the game, Jamie told herself, and jogged out onto the field, gazing around the empty stadium. Lyon was one of the few European clubs whose financial support of their women's team rivaled that of some lower tier men's teams. That was the main reason why Lyon was a guaranteed contender at Champions League nearly every year. If you invest it, they will come, as Ellie always said.

This stadium, Jamie thought, eyes flickering over the rows and rows of empty seats as she jogged around the field with her teammates, would host the 2019 World Cup final match. She pictured the seats filled, French fans painted in red and blue, American fans wearing replica jerseys and waving American flags. Would Jamie be here with the USWNT? Would Emma?

As she rounded the far goalpost, a movement in the

stadium caught her eye, and Jamie stopped dead in her tracks. *Wait.* Was that…? No, it couldn't be. And yet, it definitely was Emma moving down one of the aisles toward the field, one hand in the pocket of her familiar Sounders blue puffer coat, the other tugging her black carry-on behind her. As her eyes caught Jamie's, Emma stopped and held up a hand, smiling tiredly.

"Surprise?" she said, making it a question.

Jamie didn't hesitate. She hopped over the barrier and sprinted up the nearest aisle, cutting through an empty row to reach Emma, who had dropped her bag and was moving nearly as quickly to intercept her. They met in the middle of the row, practically slamming into each other as Jamie threw her arms around Emma and held her as tightly as she dared.

"You're here," she murmured, choking it out around the lump in her throat.

"Of course I am," Emma said, her lips warm against Jamie's cheek. "I hope that's okay?"

"Actually, on second thought," Jamie tried to joke, but the tears spilling over ruined her attempt at humor.

"Sweetie," Emma said softly, pulling back slightly to wipe Jamie's tears away.

They gazed into each other's eyes, and there was so much Jamie wanted to say to her. Deep, important things about open hearts and trust, about grand gestures and overnight flights, about the sheer relief she felt at Emma's presence beside her in the city that had long shadowed her nightmares. But before she could find the words, Seamus, Arsenal's assistant, was shouting at her, his words echoing through the empty stadium: "Right, Max, guess we'll be seeing you on your own time, then?"

Guiltily, Jamie stepped back, letting her arms drop

from Emma's waist. "Um, I think I should…" She gestured over her shoulder.

Emma nodded, smiling. "Go for it."

"We're staying at the hotel across the street—" Jamie started.

"I know," Emma interrupted. "I have a room reserved near yours. I just wanted to try to catch you before practice."

Jamie's eyes narrowed again. "Britt?"

Emma waved toward the end of the field where the goalkeepers were warming up. "Of course, Britt. Now go, before your assistant comes up here and drags you away."

Yikes. Even Seamus's ears were turning red. Jamie nodded and started to lean in to kiss Emma out of habit. At the last moment, she remembered where they were and stopped. But Emma bridged the narrow distance and kissed her softly, lingeringly.

"I'll see you after practice," she promised.

Dazed, Jamie backed away, nearly tripping over a seat. Blushing, she focused on her whereabouts enough to jog back down to field level and vault safely over the barrier. Emma was here, and she would still be here in an hour and a half. For now, Jamie owed Arsenal her focus, even if it seemed unlikely they would score two away goals and earn a shutout against a team that had averaged two goals for and zero against throughout their current Champions League campaign.

"Oi, are you sure you're ready to join us?" Seamus asked sarcastically as she jogged past him.

"I'm always ready," Jamie shot back, grinning, which earned whistles from her teammates. She risked a glance back up at the row where she'd left Emma to find her girlfriend seated and watching her.

"Good one, babe," she was pretty sure Emma mouthed at her, accompanied by a cheeky wink.

Life was good, she thought, turning back to the field. Not perfect, but Emma was here with her in Lyon. And that meant more to her than Jamie thought Emma would ever know.

CHAPTER ELEVEN

"Hey," a soft voice murmured close to Emma's ear. "Wakey, wakey, sleepy girl."

Emma twitched at the feel of lips on her forehead, and then she sat straight up, cracking her head on something hard as her surroundings filtered into view. She was in a stadium. A French stadium, judging from the signs all written in French.

"Ow," Jamie said above her, pressing a hand to her mouth and staring at Emma through wide—amused, she hoped—eyes.

Right. Lyon. Of course. Somehow, Emma had dozed off. Except it wasn't exactly a secret how she'd fallen asleep sitting in a plastic stadium chair while watching Arsenal practice. She'd barely slept on the plane the previous night. Not only had her usual fears assailed her while crossing the wide, pitch-black expanse of the Atlantic, but she had worried that Jamie wouldn't be happy to see her, despite Britt's assurances to the contrary. At least that worry had been alleviated.

Jamie pulled her hand away from her mouth, and

Emma winced as she saw her slightly swollen lower lip.

"Oh, shit," she said, rising clumsily from the seat. "Are you okay? I'm so sorry."

"That's what you get for sneaking up on her," Britt said, appearing at the end of the row. "Hey, Em!"

"Britt," Emma said, ducking past Jamie with another apologetic glance.

"I wasn't sneaking," Jamie groused as Britt and Emma hugged. "I was trying not to startle her."

"Well done," Britt deadpanned.

Emma smiled up at the goalkeeper. "Well done *you* with the secret keeping."

"I know, right? She didn't suspect a thing," Britt boasted.

"Yes, I did," Jamie said.

"No, you didn't."

"Did too."

"Did not."

"Children," Emma admonished, glancing around for her carry-on. Oh, good. It hadn't wheeled itself off without her.

Britt punched Jamie in the shoulder and then turned to sprint away, only her feet got tangled up and she nearly fell into the next row. Jamie lunged forward and caught her, and they both cracked up, wrestling (unsafely, Emma might add) as they headed back to field level.

Seriously. They really were children.

"You coming?" Jamie asked, glancing back at her.

"Duh," Emma said, and reached for her bag.

"Cranky much?" Jamie teased as they headed for the

stadium exit.

"I'm not cranky," Emma said automatically. As Britt and Jamie exchanged a look, their eyebrows raised, she added, "I can see you both, you know." Huh. Maybe they were right, given that she felt like flicking them both at full flicking strength.

"Coffee?" Jamie suggested. "They've got an espresso machine in the lobby, or there's instant in the rooms…"

"Oh my god, yes, please." Coffee sounded heavenly—not that that was anything new.

Britt snickered and then straightened quickly as Emma glanced at her with narrowed eyes. "Sorry! I'll just, uh, leave you to it." And she sped ahead, catching up to a handful of teammates who kept casting avid looks back at Emma and Jamie.

"Your friends are watching us," Emma noted as they exited onto the sidewalk outside the stadium.

"I mean, can you blame them?" Jamie asked, shaking her hair out of her eyes.

"Good point." Emma leaned in to drop a kiss on Jamie's cheek. Back in St. Louis, she'd wondered if Jamie would ever let her close enough to do that again. Now that she knew they were okay, she didn't want any space between them.

Jamie glanced at her quickly. "What was that for?"

"Nothing." Emma reached for her hand, winding their fingers together. "I just love you."

"Oh. Cool," Jamie said with a goofy smile that more than communicated her own sentiments. She squeezed Emma's hand, and they walked on together, chatting easily about Emma's flight, her game against Chicago the previous day, and Jamie's week in London.

At the hotel, Emma checked in while Jamie went back to her and Britt's room for a quick shower before dinner with the team. Emma, she'd insisted, was absolutely invited for their pre-game carbo loading at a restaurant to be named later.

When Emma had wondered aloud if the rest of the team was aware of that fact, Britt had scoffed. "Are you kidding? They can't wait for you to buy them a round." She was referencing Emma's trip to London to watch Arsenal play in the Round of Sixteen, and Emma didn't doubt she was telling the truth.

The hotel room was small but cute with a comfortable bed and, most importantly, the electric kettle and instant coffee Jamie had promised. Emma brewed a cup and took it with her into the bathroom, pausing for occasional sips as she stood under the hot spray, muscles slowly relaxing. This was good. Now that she was here, she was glad she had made the trip. Jamie's reaction made the stress of traveling back to Europe for the third time in as many months totally worth it.

Maybe they would be okay after all, she thought, remembering the look on Jamie's face as she'd sprinted up the stadium rows toward Emma: determination mixed with unquestionable relief. She'd even cried a little, and Emma's heart had broken as she'd thanked the powers that be for getting her there safely.

Surprising Jamie had definitely been the right decision.

"Yo, Em!" a voice called from the hallway, startling her. A fist pounded on the door at the same time, and after a moment, Emma sighed, turned off the water, and took another fortifying sip of coffee before reaching for her towel.

Maybe surprising Jamie had been the right decision.

"Just a minute," she called to forestall additional unnecessary noise. She hoped the team had this portion of the hotel to itself. The rest of the guests hoped that, too, even if they didn't know it yet.

She let Jamie in and returned to the bathroom for her post-shower skin care routine. It didn't take her long to get ready even though Jamie did her best to prevent her from getting dressed.

"I like you like this, though," she complained, gesturing at Emma's naked body and holding her bra just out of reach.

Emma rolled her eyes and used Jamie's notorious ticklishness to her advantage. There would be time enough for clothes-free activities later. Right now, Emma was starving and Jamie needed to join her team.

"I can be fast, though," Jamie said, trying to snag Emma's skinny jeans.

"Oh, I know you can," Emma said, and winked at her before pushing her backward onto the bed. "But I'd rather it be slow, wouldn't you?"

Jamie shifted onto her side and appeared to consider this question. "Hmm, now that you mention it…"

"Where's dinner?" Emma asked as she returned to the bathroom to apply her makeup and style her hair.

Jamie followed and leaned in the open doorway. "About that… It looks like we're not going to the restaurant next to the hotel, after all."

Her voice held a note of something that made Emma narrow in on her reflection in the mirror. "Where are we going, then?"

"Into the city," Jamie said, her eyes downcast as she fiddled with a button on her collared shirt. Despite the worry rolling off her in waves, she looked adorable in black skinny jeans, a blue shirt that matched her eyes, and white Converse high-tops. "We only have a few hours until curfew, so the team voted to explore some of the sights."

"Which sights?" Emma asked, letting her brush drop.

"The historic parts. Like one of the main squares, and I guess Vieux Lyon."

Old Lyon. According to the guide book Emma had picked up during her layover at Charles de Gaulle, Lyon's historic district bordered the neighborhood where Jamie had said her club team had been staying the night she and her buddies snuck out after curfew. And now her current teammates wanted to go exploring in that very area?

Not that any of them—other than Britt—knew of Jamie's history with the city of Lyon.

"We don't have to go with them," Emma offered. "We could grab dinner somewhere nearby and have a quiet night in, if you wanted." She wouldn't mind that herself. Going out in a foreign city with a group of people she'd only met once would be entertaining, yes, but it would also be exhausting, particularly after flying through the night.

Jamie met Emma's eyes in the mirror. "We can't. They would think I was dissing them to hang out with you."

And, yeah, that wouldn't be good teammate etiquette. Besides, if they lost tomorrow, which Jamie had assured her was likely, this would be their last night out together as a team. But Jamie had claimed she wasn't overly stressed about this trip because her team would barely be in Lyon for 24 hours and nearly all of those hours would be spent in or near the stadium. What would it mean for her if that part of the plan changed?

Emma turned away from the sink. A few steps brought her to the doorway, and she lifted one of Jamie's hands in hers, caressing the blue veins that shone through the fair skin at her wrist. "Are you sure you want to go? Like, a hundred percent certain?"

"No," Jamie admitted, her eyes on Emma's fingers making soothing circles against her skin. "But I don't think there's much of a choice. Maybe this is the perfect opportunity to face the past. I mean, you're here with me, and tomorrow's game isn't exactly high pressure." As Emma's eyebrows rose, Jamie added, "I told you, our odds of scoring multiple goals tomorrow are low, at best."

Emma tapped her wrist. "Any given day, Jamie…"

"I'm just being realistic." She rubbed her free hand through her hair. "I know you're not a big believer in fate, but I'd like to believe that I'm here at this time and place for a reason. So, yeah. I'm going to roll with it."

Jamie's soccer gods were apparently at work again. Or, to be more geographically accurate, her *football* gods.

"Would you go with them if I weren't here?" Emma asked.

"Yes, but I would be much whinier and significantly less happy about the prospect." She tugged her hand from Emma's grasp and slipped her arms around her waist, pulling her in for a hug. "I'm really glad you're here. Thank you for coming all this way."

"I'm glad I'm here too," she said, twining her arms around Jamie's neck and pressing her lips to her cheek. "And you don't have to thank me. This is what girlfriends do."

Jamie was silent for a moment, and Emma could almost hear the wheels turning in her head. Was lying (by omission, Emma attempted to remind her telepathically) also something girlfriends were supposed to do? But Jamie didn't voice the question out loud. Probably, Emma thought, she could only handle one emotional crisis at a time.

Honestly, that seemed like an excellent general rule.

#

The passenger van the taxi company provided fit the team—with a significant amount of scrunching. Emma willingly sat on Jamie's lap, enjoying the way Jamie's ears slowly reddened as they approached the city center. At least if she was distracted by the feel of Emma's breath whispering against her neck, then she wasn't thinking about the last time she had been to this city only a few months before they'd met.

Twelve years. They had known each other for twelve years. At some level, Emma had loved Jamie for every single one of those years. God, they'd wasted so much time. How many more years would they have to wait to live in the same city, let alone share a home? But at least they were together now. And for the first time since the football gods had deigned to bring them back into each other's lives, they were both official members of the national team.

Appreciate what you have while you have it, Emma reminded herself, breathing in Jamie's scent as the players chatted and the van crossed a low bridge over a wide river—the Rhône, Emma believed—and then turned to follow the river into the city. Their athletic careers were as impermanent and unguaranteed as their bodies were fallible. Their relationship wasn't impervious, either. At any point, one of them could tire of the challenge of what was essentially a long-distance relationship and call it quits. Well, Emma probably wouldn't. But Jamie was younger and had never experienced the maelstrom of the World Cup. There was no way to prepare for the tumult that surrounded the most important tournament in the world.

You just had to get through it.

Kind of like tonight.

She could feel Jamie tensing beside her as the van turned at last from the river and headed into the narrow streets of the 1st arrondissement where, according to Jamie's teammate (Anya? or was it Angela?), "the best, most authentic Lyonnaise bouchon" could be found. Also, the restaurant was run by all women, a fact Anya/Angela had thought they might appreciate.

"You okay?" Emma murmured in Jamie's ear.

"Fine," she said, but Emma wasn't buying it.

"It's not too late to go back to the hotel and make sweet, sweet love," she offered.

Jamie's shoulders shook as she tried to stifle a giggle.

"Hey, no secrets, Americanos," Jeanie, the striker who had given Emma a hard time in London a few months earlier, called from the row behind them.

"Sorry," Jamie replied sassily, and tightened her grip on Emma's waist. "Thanks," she added softly.

"Anytime," Emma said. "And I mean anytime, Jamie..."

"Shush." Jamie wasn't quite smiling, but Emma would take it.

The van dropped them off in a section of the city that seemed more rundown than she would have expected. Many of the shop fronts had for rent signs and/or were peppered with spray paint. As they set off along the narrow street, Emma was glad the sun was still out for a few more hours. She took Jamie's hand in hers, fully prepared not to let go until—well, maybe not until warm-up for the following day's match. Jamie glanced at her gratefully and held on tight even after they reached the restaurant whose neatly painted exterior and elegant sign was noticeably at odds with the rest of the neighborhood.

The interior was just as unexpected. Rustic exposed beams, red-painted walls, and dark wood décor created a warm and inviting ambience, and the wait staff was friendly even in the face of the cadre of hungry, English-speaking athletes. Fortunately, it was still early for dinner by French standards, and Anya (it was Anya, Jamie had confirmed) had called ahead for a reservation. They were soon seated at a row of square tables that had been pressed together along one side of the dining room. It took a while to order, but the appetizers—salad, hearty bread with olive oil and balsamic, and pumpkin soup—tided everyone over nicely, as did multiple bottles of red wine.

As the meal wore on, Emma was glad to see that Jamie seemed to be enjoying herself. Dinner was as rowdy as their pub visit before the Arsenal-United match had been in November, all jokes and loud voices and louder laughter with the addition of the occasional subtle flinging of food. Emma was content once again to sit back and watch Jamie goof around with Britt and their Arsenal friends, several of whom would be playing for their respective national teams in Canada this summer.

Midway through the meal, she caught Amelia Brown, the English national team's leading scorer and longtime captain, eyeing her from across the table, mouth pursed in a thin line. Or maybe that was just her resting bitch face. Hard to tell, really.

"What?" Emma asked, feeling her chin jut upward automatically at the challenge in the other woman's eyes.

"I wasn't offsides," Amelia said.

Emma knew exactly what she was referring to, but she cocked her head to one side. "Against Lyon? Sorry, I didn't see that game."

Amelia huffed. "In February. I was even with Wall and you know it. That match should have been a tie."

Jamie had mentioned that AB, as the team called her, was still hot under the collar about the offsides call that had given the US the win against England earlier in the year. Emma only shrugged. "I can't help you there. Referees are human, you know?"

"So you admit it," AB said, her brown eyes glinting.

"Knock it off, AB," Jamie said, sliding back into her seat beside Emma. She'd left momentarily to "return" a piece of roll to its rightful owner at a nearby table. Now she stared evenly at the English national team captain. "Emma is here as an Arsenal fan, not as a US player. Right, babe?"

Emma winced. An Arsenal fan? Hardly. "I'm here to support your Champions League run, totally."

Jamie's amused side-eye told Emma her verbal maneuvering had been duly noted.

"Fine," AB said, leaning back. "Congrats on making the US roster, by the way."

"Thanks," Emma said. "Your roster is looking solid. How's the support been from your federation?"

The previous tension dissipated as they compared notes on the status of the women's game in their home countries. Amelia had been one of the European stars to sign on to the failed lawsuit against FIFA to force Canada to provide grass fields for World Cup matches. Like Emma, she had been disappointed when FIFA pulled every legal trick in the book to avoid having to address the players' concerns.

"But at least 2019 will be all grass," Amelia said, shrugging as she carved a slice off her broiled chicken and popped it in her mouth.

"Right. That's something," Emma agreed.

The conversation paused, and she wondered if Jamie and Amelia were asking themselves the same question she was currently entertaining: *Will I still be playing in 2019?* They would probably all still be playing professionally, but internationally was a different matter. Emma and Jamie needed to perform well in Canada both individually and collectively, as a team, in order to avoid a coaching or lineup change that would threaten their spots. Amelia, however, was already in her early thirties. Emma doubted she would still be leading the English side four years down the road. Then again, she didn't seem to be slowing down. Maybe she would beat the odds and play longer.

"All right, all right, all right!" Jeanie called out a little while later after the post-entrée cheese course had been devoured. "We have four hours until curfew. Who wants to go exploring?"

While the rest of the team cheered, Emma glanced at Jamie, who was frowning slightly. "Whatever you want to do," Emma said quietly, "I'm fine with."

"I don't know," Jamie admitted, her voice low. "It's weird being here. Not as in *here*," she added, gesturing around the restaurant, "but out there."

Emma knew the bar where the assault had happened was located near where the Rhône and the city's smaller river, the Saône, met. She'd checked her phone for their location when they'd arrived and had discovered that the restaurant was a few miles north of the confluence—not that that meant anything, necessarily. She took Jamie's hand again. "We could always head back to the hotel. Blame me if you want."

Jamie smiled at her, pressing Emma's fingers with her own. "You said once that I was too good to you. Well, ditto, Blake."

If only that were true, Emma thought. But she smiled back at Jamie anyway.

Outside, the light overhead had taken on a yellowish tint. Somewhere beyond the rows and rows of buildings, the sun was beginning to set. Britt fell into step on Jamie's other side as Anya guided the group down one of the cramped streets that led away from the restaurant. To what, Emma had no idea. But Jamie didn't seem inclined to call for a cab just yet.

"How you doing?" Britt asked, leaning into Jamie's shoulder.

"I'm okay," Jamie told her. "It's strange being here, I'm not going to lie. But it's different from how I remember it."

"In what way?" Emma asked.

"It's brighter, for one," Jamie admitted. "In my memory, everything is darker and smaller, warped somehow."

That made sense to Emma—trauma could impact the mind in powerful ways. But she didn't say as much to Jamie. Probably, she didn't have to.

"Let me know if you need anything," Britt said.

"Thanks, man."

They bumped fists, and Emma hid a smile at their bro-like behavior. It was sweet that Britt had her back, too. Or rather, her other side. Jamie had her own honor guard to escort her through the city tonight.

A few blocks from the restaurant was a wide, rectangular square—Place des Terreaux, according to the signs—bordered by shops and restaurants on one side, a highly ornamented building that reminded Emma of a palace on another, and an art museum on yet another. Near the shops, a prototypical Western European fountain contained an intricate sculpture of a half-naked lady guiding a chariot pulled by four wild horses.

Emma sighed, wishing she had her guide book. Unfortunately, it hadn't fit in her purse.

"Here," Jamie said, offering Emma her phone. "I've probably got more data left on my international plan than you do."

"Oh. Thanks," Emma said, toying with her ponytail as she accepted the phone.

Soon she was reading the relevant Wikipedia entry aloud to Jamie and Britt, who listened politely as she informed them that they were looking at the Fontaine Bartholdi, named for the artist who had sculpted the fountain's centerpiece in 1892 out of 21 tons of lead. The female charioteer represented the nation of France while the four horses symbolized the country's four great rivers. Why France needed to be a half-naked woman was not mentioned in the article, but in Emma's experience, this seemed like a reasonable representation of the European nation.

"Wait," Jamie said, gazing up at the fountain. "Bartholdi designed the Statue of Liberty, didn't he?"

Emma did a quick Google search. "Yes! Good memory."

"Child of an artist," Jamie said.

"An artist in your own right," Britt insisted, sliding her arm around Jamie's neck and giving her a noogie, albeit a gentle one. Laughing, Jamie shoved her away.

"Oh," Emma said, still scrolling through the phone.

"What?"

"It says here that Place des Terreaux was the site of

public beheadings."

Jamie and Britt glanced around the wide open space occupied by tourists of varying nationalities, and Emma wondered if, like her, they were having a difficult time imagining scenes of violent spectacle. Once again, she was glad to live when she did—even if it meant she had a fairly solid shot at being present at the end of the world.

They wandered the square for a little while with other visitors out on the warm spring evening, snapping pictures at the fountain and posing in front of the ornate seventeenth century Hôtel de Ville, which wasn't actually a hotel but rather Lyon's City Hall. Emma kept an eye on Jamie as they walked. She must have been here before with her club team given that the square was apparently considered the center of the large city. But she seemed relaxed for now, and Emma didn't want to change that by being overly solicitous.

From the square, the group headed down yet another narrow street. But this one was wider, mostly graffiti-free, and sported upscale grocers as well as shops like The North Face and Vans. Jamie and Britt kept pausing to admire intricately carved wooden doors set beside the glass windows of modern storefronts, but Emma walked on, reading more about their current surroundings. At least this street didn't feel quite as ominous, probably because there was a light at the end. Literally, since they were walking toward the sun setting over the—Emma checked the phone's GPS—Saône River.

At the intersection, they crossed the Quai de la Pêcherie and began to walk south along the river, the sun hanging just over the slopes of Fourvière Hill crowned by the ornate towers of the nineteenth century basilica, Lyon's very own Notre Dame. The breeze off the water was cool, and Emma leaned into Jamie's side, grateful for her heat.

Despite the potential emotional landmines lurking beneath the streets of Lyon, being with Jamie like this was nice. They weren't teammates here, so there were no team time rules to worry about. Even if there had been, Jamie's commitment to Arsenal was set to expire the following day (assuming they lost), and she'd already said she didn't intend to sign on again next season. With the Summer Olympics on the docket, she didn't want another crazy year ping-ponging between Arsenal, the Thorns, and the national team—a decision Emma fully supported.

A block down the Quai, Anya gestured at a corner building across the street. "Notice anything about that building?"

At first Emma didn't. But then her mind caught up with her eyes, and she gasped slightly. What she had thought were windows were actually painted on. One entire side of the six-story building was smooth stone painted to look as if giant, colorful books occupied the building's windows and window ledges.

"Holy crap," Emma heard Jamie murmur.

"It's called the City Library," Anya told them, clearly enjoying the amazed looks on her teammates' faces.

Emma had read about Lyon's murals on the flight from Paris. There were 50 or 60 of these paintings about the city, dreamed up in the 1970s by an art collective as a way to brighten up and rejuvenate industrial Lyon's public spaces. If she remembered correctly, the largest mural in the city, La Fresque des Lyonnais, was somewhere nearby. She checked the phone surreptitiously. Yep, only a few blocks up the riverbank.

After they'd gawked at the enormous books and other images painted on the side of the building, Anya led them up the Quai to an almost triangular-shaped building set apart from its neighbors. La Fresque des Lyonnais had been painted to resemble a typical Lyonnais scene, only with more than two dozen famous city residents, past and present, added in. Google helpfully informed them that the mural included the Roman emperor Claudius, who had been born there when Lyon was still part of Roman Gaul; Antoine de Saint-Exupéry, author of *The Little Prince*; Lyonnais filmmakers, silk weavers, chefs, and others all posing on their painted-on balconies. All in all, the mural occupied 8,600 square feet of the building's surface, exactly twice the size of the nearby City Library fresco.

"I must not have seen this before," Jamie told Emma, her eyes shining and her voice wondering as she stared up at the warm, colorful mural. "I would have remembered something this incredible."

"I'm sure you would have." Emma slid her arm around Jamie's waist and rested her chin on her shoulder. She was really, really glad she'd changed her plane ticket.

The sun was nearly down, the sky overhead streaked with gray and pink clouds when Anya led them across a pedestrian suspension bridge over the Saône River to Old Lyon. Jamie gripped her hand tighter as they reached the far shore but otherwise appeared unaffected as they left the river behind and entered a maze of cobblestoned streets. Like other European cities Emma had visited, this section of Lyon, constructed during the Renaissance, felt archaic. Fifteenth and sixteenth century tower blocks that seemed more Italian than French rose straight up on either side of the road that had clearly been built before the invention of automobiles. Emma, who handled small spaces about as well as the next person, felt a touch claustrophobic as they passed picturesque French shops that sold silk scarves, vintage electric bikes, and lots and lots of cheese. For some reason, there were also numerous English style pubs in Lyon's oldest neighborhood. This seemed particularly odd given that Emma's guide book had indicated that the second most populous city in France was known as the gastronomic center of the foodie nation.

They didn't stop at any of the bars, English or otherwise. Instead they visited a bakery just before it closed and picked out dessert. Tomorrow, after all, was game day. While wine and beer with dinner were expected of a group of European footballers, going out the night before a game to an establishment designed to get its customers inebriated was not on the to-do list. Even if it had been, Emma was fairly certain she and Jamie would have abstained.

Dessert, however, they had no intention of abstaining from. As the bakery staff cleaned the empty seating area, Emma and Jamie selected a salted caramel tart to share. Then they continued their stroll, licking the sweet salty goodness from their fingers and kissing the crumbs from each other's mouths. In the darkening streets, with exterior lights only just beginning to flicker on, most people appeared as silhouettes passing over the cobblestones.

"They probably think I'm a guy," Jamie murmured as they passed a group of tourists who didn't even blink at their public display of affection.

Probably, Emma thought. But she only shrugged and kissed the corner of Jamie's mouth again. It was nice to be anonymous in Europe again, away from the worries of rosters, sponsors, and team rules. At least for a little while.

Just before the last light faded from the sky, Anya led them to the building across from a courthouse with life-sized statues of human figures who looked like they were about to jump out of the windows on whose ledges they stood. Smirking over her shoulder, Anya pulled a heavy wooden door open and gestured them forward.

"What's this, now?" AB asked.

"A secret passageway," Anya said as if the answer were obvious. "The locals call it a *traboule*. They let you pass from one street to the next. You have to be quiet, though, so you don't bother the people who live here."

As the team discussed the secret passageway amongst themselves, Emma surreptitiously checked Jamie's phone. Google confirmed that Anya was correct. This *traboule* was the longest one in the city, and offered passage through four different sixteenth century buildings and courtyards between Rue Saint-Jean and Rue du Boeuf.

"Well?" Anya prodded, looking around at the group. "You guys going to wuss out or what?"

Jeanie stepped up to the doorway. "Why not? If anything goes wrong, at least I won't have to see the smug mugs of the Frenchies tomorrow."

"You in?" Britt asked Jamie.

She paused. "Yeah. Let's do it."

Emma stayed close to Jamie as they entered the passageway not because she was worried about her but because Emma had done the Seattle Underground Tour with her family as a preteen, and the guide's tales of ghosts and bubonic plague still haunted her. Fortunately, the dark, cramped passageway soon opened into a square courtyard that offered a tiny slice of sky four or five flights up. There were other tourists admiring the view, but Jamie's teammates didn't pause. Anya led them into another corridor that was wider and more interesting than the previous one, with multiple arches and triangular sconces that leant the passage a medieval feel. The stone walls were smooth and Emma had no problem imagining the ancient city's silk workers carrying their goods through the passageway between buildings on their way to market.

After passing through more courtyards and corridors

of differing architectural styles, they eventually came out on Rue du Boeuf (Street of the Beef, they translated, snickering). A couple of blocks later, they bought tickets at the Vieux Lyon train station to the funicular train that would take them to the top of Fourvière Hill, where the Basilique Notre Dame de Fourvière stood sentry over the city. They could have taken the stairs up from Rue du Boeuf, but they'd decided collectively that climbing 800 stairs the night before Champions League semis was probably not the best idea. The train ride was short but the sky was fully dark by the time they reached the hill's crest. Fortunately, hundreds of lights lit up the exterior of Lyon's Notre Dame and the surrounding area.

Emma stood beside Jamie at a low stone wall looking out over the flickering lights of the city hundreds of feet below, the imposing basilica at their back. Frankly, she was glad to have escaped the ancient streets and medieval buildings of Old Lyon. Historic sites were awesome and all, but she preferred that her UNESCO World Heritage sites have wide open skies.

"It's beautiful," Jamie murmured, and reached for her hand.

Automatically Emma started to glance around, assessing who may or may not be watching them, but then she stopped and moved closer to Jamie. "It really is."

The city was spread out before them, the many bridges easy to pick out, building facades along the rivers almost as visible as they would be in daylight. There was certainly no shortage of lights in Lyon.

Jamie pointed out a giant Ferris wheel visible in a huge square on the peninsula between the two rivers. "I went up in that when I was here before," she said, smiling. "It's super high—a couple hundred feet tall, I think."

That really was high. Emma tried not to make a face at

the thought of hanging out in open space so far above what was likely an unforgiving cobblestone surface. Jamie was recalling a pleasant memory from her previous trip here, and Emma didn't want to burst her bubble. But as Jamie cast her a sideways smile, she realized she had probably failed to achieve that particular objective.

"Sorry, guys," Anya said at that moment, turning away from the view, "but curfew is approaching. There are a couple of options here. We can tour the church—it has amazing art, by the way—or check out the Roman ruins on the way down the hill. Or we can split up and you can figure out your own way home."

Part of the group voted to tour the church while others decided to start down the hill. Still others decided to wander off on their own, which was how Emma and Jamie found themselves a little while later at the ruins of a Gallo-Roman amphitheater only a five minute walk from the church. They had actually joined the church tour at first because Jamie wanted to see the mosaics and stained glass the basilica was famous for, but they'd said goodnight to Britt and slipped away once they'd gazed their fill at the church's ornate interior.

On their way out of the hilltop complex, they'd stopped briefly to admire a partial replica of the Eiffel Tower, noting how much the metal design contrasted with the church's four towers and the massive gilded statue of the Virgin Mary standing atop a separate bell tower. Then, with only an hour to spare before curfew, they'd headed down the hill to explore the city's Roman ruins, dating back more than two thousand years to when Lyon had served as the capital of Roman Gaul.

The Ancient Theatre of Fourvière, which Jamie's phone said had been renovated in the 20th century, was situated on the side of the hill overlooking the city.

Plentiful lamps and spotlights made the ruins, like the church, visible both from the city below and to tourists interested in exploring the complex after the sun had set and the crowds had dissipated.

"Do you want to…?" Jamie gestured at the rows upon rows of seats just below them that overlooked the half-circle stage.

"Totally," Emma said. "Do we have time, though?"

"I mean, what's the worst that can happen if we're a little late?"

"Seamus would yell at us?"

"Pretty sure you've faced worse."

"Yes, but have you?" Emma teased as they started down the well-lit stairs that led to the theater complex.

"I never had to play for Jeff Bradbury, so no," Jamie replied.

"Count yourself lucky," Emma said, making a face at the memory of the national team coach before Marty.

When they reached the amphitheater, they picked their way gingerly down a steep aisle to a row in the center of the curved seating area well out of earshot of the dozen or so other people exploring the ruins after-hours.

"I wish we could see this in daylight," Emma commented as they sat down together. She leaned into Jamie for warmth, glad she'd packed her winter jacket for Chicago. She almost hadn't—it had been 75 in Chicago the previous week—but a late cold snap had convinced her it wouldn't hurt to bring it along at least. Good thing, because 50 degrees felt colder than it should when you were seated on an ancient stone bench.

"I wish a lot of things," Jamie said after a moment. Her voice was weighted with more emotion than usual, and

Emma could feel the questions coming even before Jamie voiced them: "Why didn't you tell me you were being harassed? Was it really just to keep me from getting knocked off my game, or was there something else?"

So much for dealing with one emotional crisis at a time.

Emma turned to face her, steeling herself for the difficult conversation. She'd had plenty of time since St. Louis to talk through her actions and motivations with her mom on the phone and Dani in person. Probably, they had each counseled, it would be best to be as honest as possible from here on out.

"Both," she admitted, resisting the urge to touch the side of Jamie's face that was hidden in shadows. "I really was worried about throwing you off your game, but there was more to it than that. You asked before if this was what Tyler was talking about. If you're willing to listen, I'd like to tell you what happened with Sam. Not to excuse what I did but to explain the context."

Jamie nodded. "Okay. I'm listening."

Even though she'd been expecting that answer, Emma still hesitated as she tried to determine the best way to start the story. Finally, she said, "So there was this guy on Twitter a few years ago who kept trying to get me to meet him in real life."

Jamie stayed quiet as Emma explained how the photo of Sam at the 2011 World Cup quarterfinals in her Blakeley jersey had set off Emma's "admirer," how he had switched his focus to Sam, how he had tweeted increasingly violent messages to her, how they had finally met with a police officer who suggested they basically go underground to ensure their online harasser didn't come after them in real life. Oh, and maybe buy a gun so they could shoot him in self-defense if he did show up at one of their apartments.

"She broke up with me that night, and I don't blame her," Emma said, shrugging as she looked down at the bench in shadows between them. "I genuinely don't know how she could have stayed after that."

"Wow," Jamie said. "That's so fucked up. I just… *Jesus*, Emma."

"See?" Emma said, throwing her hands into the air. "That's the reaction I was trying to avoid. Because after that comes the, 'It's not you, it's me,' speech, and then our friends are pissed at us and we lose the World Cup and everyone blames us…"

"Hold on," Jamie said, shaking her head at Emma's dramatics. "That's not going to happen. For one thing, I'm not about to launch into that clichéd speech."

She squinted up at Jamie through her eyelashes. "You're not?"

"Of course not."

"Oh, thank god. After the Tori Parker fiasco, I don't think my national team career could survive another teammate break-up."

"You're not wrong," Jamie agreed. "But seriously, I can't believe that asshole threatened Sam like that. It must have been terrifying for you both. What is wrong with people?"

"They're generally assholes?" Emma suggested.

"You don't really believe that."

She looked away, eyes on the city lights in the distance. "I don't know. I'm not sure I see compelling evidence to the contrary."

"I'm so sorry that happened to you guys," Jamie said softly, reaching for her hands and holding them, her warmth immediately seeping into Emma's skin.

"Thanks." Her shoulders relaxed as she realized Jamie really wasn't going to break up with her now that she knew the full truth. At least, not right away.

"Hey." Jamie released one of her hands and touched Emma's chin instead, turning it gently until their eyes met. "Did you really think I would walk away from you, from us, over something like that?"

"I didn't—I wasn't—" Emma started, but then she stopped. That was exactly what she had worried about: that she and Jamie, too, would end up in a rundown police station with a semi-disinterested officer recommending they change their addresses, their driver's licenses, their entire lives because some entitled bastard they'd never met had decided Emma owed him herself. That Jamie, too, would decide it was too much; that she wouldn't think Emma was worth the risk.

"I'm not her," Jamie said, her thumb smoothing across Emma's cheek. "I'm in the public eye as much as you are, and I don't know if you've noticed this, but I have my own trolls to deal with. We can't let them come between us, Em. I have to believe we're stronger than that—and so do you. There's so much ahead of us, both good and bad. That's the nature of the lives we've chosen. But you have to believe that we can survive almost anything, or we're not going to make it."

Because if you don't believe you can do something, you probably won't be able to do it.

Emma sighed, leaning into Jamie's hand cupping her cheek. "I know. I'm sorry I let you down. I really am."

"It's okay," Jamie said. "We don't have to be perfect. We just have to be able to handle whatever comes at us. Preferably together. Agreed?"

She nodded and moved closer, burying her face in

Jamie's jacket. "Agreed. I love you, you know."

"I love you too," Jamie murmured, her lips warm against Emma's forehead.

Her mind told her to crack a joke about how she must love Jamie, since she was snuggling against an Arsenal jacket, but she shushed it. Now was not the time to make light of the challenges facing them—especially not with the World Cup looming in the near distance.

They stayed on the cold stone bench longer than they really should have, holding onto each other and talking quietly in the amphitheater that had been built to function in an epically different world. By unspoken agreement, they stuck to impersonal topics like the kinds of events the theater complex might have hosted over its long history, from gladiator fights and poetry readings—"Sappho, anyone?" Jamie joked—to Shakespearean tragedies and comedies. Nowadays, Lyon hosted an international festival each summer called Fourvière Nights that, over the course of eight weeks, brought circus shows, theatre acts, movies, dance performances, and musical concerts to the ancient amphitheater's stage.

"Maybe," Jamie said, her tone noticeably casual, "we should come back sometime and check out the festival."

Emma pulled away so that she could better see Jamie's expression. "Wait. You would come back here willingly? Like, without a game of some kind to compel you to do so?"

"In theory? Absolutely."

"You don't mind being here, then?" Emma pressed.

"Actually, it's kind of anticlimactic, to be honest. I was a kid when I was here before, and the city genuinely doesn't seem familiar. I don't know if I've just blocked it out, but whatever the reason, coming here hasn't been the drama fest I thought it would be."

"Well, that's good," Emma said, leaning closer again.

"Maybe it's because you're here," Jamie added, her voice soft again. "I really do appreciate what you did to get here. I know it couldn't have been easy."

"Seriously. Flying first class on a trip to France in the springtime is definitely rough."

"Jerk," Jamie said, and started to pull away.

But Emma didn't let her. She held her close, nuzzling her neck. "So you really don't hate me for screwing things up?"

Jamie huffed slightly, but she didn't try to hide her smile. "Not completely, I guess."

Emma smacked her shoulder, and then leaned her head onto the spot she had just abused. "And this is a good surprise, then?"

Jamie tugged her closer. "The best surprise. Not *ever*, because the London vacation still has that covered."

"Obviously," Emma said. Because, duh. Then: "Thanks, Jamie."

"For what?"

For still being my girlfriend, she thought. "For letting me be here," she said aloud, purposely leaving the meaning of *here* open to interpretation.

"You're welcome. Thanks for being here." And she kissed Emma sweetly there in Lyon's two thousand year old ruins.

A little while later, Emma commented, "Want to upgrade to first class and ride home with me tomorrow?"

"Totally," Jamie said without any hesitation at all.

"Awesome," Emma said, smiling at the view of the

city spread out before them.

For the first time since St. Louis, she could see a future with Jamie again, which told her that her decision to fly to France had absolutely been the right decision. She would make a hundred lonely night flights across the world if Jamie needed her to. In truth, though, as they sat quietly together watching the lights of Lyon from a safe distance, she was just as happy she wouldn't have to.

Jamie was right about one thing: They wouldn't be the reason the US team lost this summer because the US was going to WIN the World Cup, and afterward Emma and Jamie were going to fly off alone together to an island in the Caribbean or some other remote location where they could sleep late and eat whatever they wanted and just be themselves—two women who had been in love with each other for what felt like, and truly might be, forever.

The fantasy, which Emma let herself engage in often when she and Jamie were apart, was sweet. But before they could disappear to that imagined island paradise free of stress and expectations, they had a fair bit of work ahead of them. Summer was coming, and Emma was ready for it.

So, she was pretty sure, was Jamie.

ABOUT THE AUTHOR

Kate Christie, author of twelve novels including *Beautiful Game*, *Leaving LA*, *Gay Pride & Prejudice*, and the Girls of Summer series, lives near Seattle with her wife, three young daughters, and the family dog. A graduate of Smith College and Western Washington University, Kate has played soccer most of her life and counts attending the 2015 World Cup finals game in Vancouver as one of her top five *Favorite. Days. Ever.*

To read excerpts from Kate's other titles from Second Growth Books and Bella Books, please visit her author website at www.katejchristie.com. Or check out her blog, *Homodramatica* at katechristie.wordpress.com, where she occasionally finds time to wax unpoetically about lesbian life, fiction, and motherhood.

To receive updates on the next book in the Girls of Summer series, visit Kate's blog and sign up for her mailing list at katechristie.wordpress.com/mailing-list.

Printed in Great Britain
by Amazon